THE ATLANTIS ASCENT

BOOK 7 OF THE ATLANTIS SAGA

S.A. BECK

ISBN-13: 978-1987859591

ISBN-10: 1987859596

CHAPTER 1

AUGUST 17, 2016, THE DESERT THIRTY
MILES EAST OF TIMBUKTU, MALI
7:30 P.M.

It had all been going too slowly for Jaxon Ares
Anderson. As the sun grew red and swollen over the
sand dunes to the west, she felt as if she had been
living these past few days forever.

She had been in a gunfight on the outskirts of
Timbuktu, nearly lost her life more than once, saved
her boyfriend from kidnapping, and seen a good
friend die with her own eyes.

Brett Lawson was supposed to have already been
dead. Her old classmate and partner in crime
fighting had come back from supposedly being

murdered in Los Angeles and tried to kill her with the speed and strength of an Atlantean. Instead, he was the one who'd gotten killed, taken down in a hailstorm of bullets fired by her companions in the Atlantis Allegiance.

They had made it out of Timbuktu one step ahead of the law before she ditched them to go back and see the Atlantean community there.

And now she was in a car speeding across the Sahara Desert with a team of Atlanteans, or People of the Sea, as the locals called them, although the people with her were not locals. While they spoke English, and they all had the broad Asian faces, black skin, and sparkling blue eyes typical of her people. Those same features had set her apart for so long, but now she felt right at home. She had found a whole community of Atlanteans.

They called themselves the Atlantis Guard and said they were part of a global organization fighting to protect their people. The four of them came from various countries and were all in their late twenties.

She had told them to take her back to her friends. She felt bad about leaving them and knew they must be worried sick about her. The problem was, she had only a vague idea where they were, and since they were trying to avoid the cops, they sure hadn't stayed put.

Had it only been a few months ago that she was a messed-up kid flunking every subject at school and talking back to her foster parents? The chain of events that had brought her to this point was incredible. She'd discovered she was part of a hidden race from a lost continent, a race that a secret faction in the United States government wanted to use as guinea pigs. And now the Russians were after them too. She'd spent seventeen years being ignored and put down, and now suddenly she was the center of all this attention, none of it good.

"Penny for your thoughts," said the Atlantean sitting beside her. His name was Winston Chambers, and he was from England. He had plucked her off the streets of Timbuktu and probably saved her from getting arrested.

He had also dropped the biggest bombshell of this entire trip—he had known her parents. They had lived in London, like Winston, and had fled because a criminal gang wanted to use their Atlantean powers for its own ends. Her mother and father had settled for a time in Portland, where Jaxon had been born, but the gangsters caught up with them. Jaxon had been given up for adoption at the last minute, just before her parents got killed.

And if she wasn't careful, she'd join them.

"I was just thinking about all this mess and not knowing how to fix it," Jaxon said, looking out at the brown expanse of the Sahara. No buildings or other vehicles were in sight. The only sign of civilization was the track on which they drove, cut into the sand by countless other trucks and cars that had passed before them.

Winston chuckled. "If only I knew how to fix all this myself."

"Tell me more about my parents."

"In time—we have a getaway to perform."

"No, now. If I've learned one thing on this trip, it's that I can die at any time. I'm not going to die without finally finding out about my parents."

He looked over at Trisha, an Atlantean from the United States, who sat on the other side of Jaxon in the back seat. Two more Atlanteans sat in front.

Trisha nodded, and Winston began to speak.

"As I mentioned to you in Timbuktu, your parents were Keepers of the Texts. Like the griots of the Sahara, they are the guardians of heritage and learning. Your mother and father knew some of the original knowledge of our lost continent. Not just anyone can become one of the Keepers of the Texts. I can't, and no one else in this car can. It runs in the blood, passed from parents to children since the days of the sinking of Atlantis. You are the only one we know of, which is why we have been searching for you for so long. You are special. Besides the individual power each Atlantean enjoys, you have an additional power. You can sense the old places of learning and magic."

"Yes, but what were they like?"

"Your parents? Scholarly, intelligent, kind."

Jaxon laughed. "All the things I'm not."

Trisha nudged her as if she was a naughty younger sister. "Don't shortchange yourself."

"I'm dyslexic and get crap grades at school. I'm not very smart, and I bite people's heads off if they cross me."

Winston shrugged. "Most of that is because you're an orphan. I bet you went through a dozen foster homes with an endless parade of bad foster parents—disciplinarians, perverts, religious nuts. I've met them all. The British foster system is no better than the American foster system."

"Try the orphanages in Peru," the man at the wheel said. He spoke with a Hispanic accent. "I'm

Mateo, by the way. Nobody here really likes me, but they keep me around because I'm a great shot."

"Um, happy to meet you, Mateo," Jaxon said.

"Mateo has been through a lot. We all love him, but you have to be patient with him," Trisha said then motioned to the woman in the passenger seat. "Elaine and I were lucky. We actually grew up with parents."

Elaine laughed. When she spoke, it was with a slow Southern drawl. "No, you're the lucky one, New York City girl. Any mutt can fit in in that place. Me, I grew up in Mississippi, which meant all the white folks assumed I was black and treated me accordingly."

"Been there, done that," Jaxon grumbled.

"We've all been through hell and high water," Winston said. "But let's not get bitter, shall we? I spent a few years doing that, and it didn't help. Besides, we have a mission to accomplish."

Jaxon nodded and looked out the window again. "It's going to get dark soon. We need to find my friends, or we'll have to camp out here alone tonight."

While Jaxon had felt an immediate sense of trust with these people, just like with the Atlantean community in Timbuktu, being separated from the Atlantis Allegiance left her with an ache in her heart. She hadn't realized until now just how attached she had become to all of them.

"Time to break out the hardware," Elaine said. "Mateo, find someplace we can park without being seen by anyone passing by."

Mateo got off the track they were driving on and soon found a series of low sand dunes. He wove the Land Rover between them until they got to a spot out of sight of the surrounding countryside.

Once Mateo parked, Elaine got out and opened up the back, humming a cheerful tune. Jaxon got out, too, curious to see what she was up to. Already, the scorching desert air had begun to lose its power. In less than an hour, the sun would set, and the temperature would plunge. There was nothing to hold in the heat in this empty land.

Elaine pulled out a small crate and opened it to reveal a drone set in Styrofoam packing. It was a little more than a foot in diameter, and as the Southerner pulled it out, Jaxon could see a camera on the bottom.

"How in the world did you sneak that into the country?" Jaxon asked.

"Winston is a handy guy to have around."

Jaxon remembered how he had hypnotized a policeman who had tried to arrest them back in

Timbuktu and nodded. It must have been quite a sight to watch that mild-mannered Englishman pull that off at the airport security check.

Elaine set the drone on the ground, took out a remote control that had a small view screen on it, and flipped a switch.

The drone came to life. Like an oversized insect, it buzzed up into the air and was soon nothing more than a dot overhead. Elaine pushed a button, and the screen came on, showing a remarkably clear picture of the surrounding desert. The Land Rover appeared as a little rectangle below with two dots next to it.

"Wave to the camera," Elaine said with a grin. She turned a joystick, and the camera panned around. Far off in one direction appeared a column of dust.

"That's them!" Jaxon said.

"Nope. You said your folks only have two vehicles. See how thick and long that dust trail is? That's half a dozen at least. Must be one of the patrols out looking for us. At least they're not headed directly for us. They're moving for that ridge to the west."

"Think they've spotted something?"

"Perhaps. Let's take a look."

The view shifted as the drone rose and zipped to

the west. The ridge came into clearer view. Beyond it, the sun sparked off two vehicles.

"Bingo," Elaine said. "I don't think your friends know they're being followed. That ridge is high enough they might not see the dust trail."

Jaxon tensed. "Can we get there in time?"

"We better."

They leaped back in the car, and Mateo slammed on the gas.

As the Land Rover tore through the desert, Mateo kept looking in the rearview mirror. The dust trail was clearly visible behind them, looming on the horizon like a storm cloud.

"They're going to see us for sure," Mateo said.

Jaxon shook her head. "It doesn't matter as long as we get there first. We can head off together, and once it's dark, they won't be able to find us."

Mateo's reflection grinned at her. "Well, you're cool under pressure. Remind me to teach you how to shoot."

"I'm not really into guns. My boyfriend is a big gun nut, though."

Mateo looked a bit disappointed at the mention of a boyfriend. Jaxon snorted. Guys were always guys, even if they were Atlanteans.

"Look, another dust column to the south," Trisha said. "They're really after us."

"It's my fault," Jaxon admitted. "I spoke with Salif, one of our people in Timbuktu, and he said the cops are asking the community all sorts of questions about me and my friends. We got in a gunfight with the Russian agents a couple of days ago and left a bunch of them dead. An ... American got killed too."

Jaxon paused. Should she tell them about Brett, how her friend had been turned into some human-Atlantean hybrid by General Meade's secret faction in the US government? So many facts and plots were buzzing around in her head she didn't know how to think straight.

Mateo banged his fist against the steering wheel. "It's always the same. The first sign of trouble, and they blame our people."

"Look at it from the cops' perspective," Trisha said. "All they see is two groups of foreigners shooting up their town, and one of the groups has an Atlantean along. Of course they're going to be suspicious of us."

"You're always making excuses for them," Mateo griped. Jaxon got the impression that when he said "them," he meant normal humans.

"Let's just get back to my friends. They'll be worried sick about me," Jaxon said.

The driver caught her eye in the rearview mirror. "You're better off without their kind."

Jaxon bit her lip. Yes, he definitely meant regular humans.

Nevertheless, he handled the Land Rover like an expert, careening between sand dunes and speeding across the flat portions. The ridge loomed ahead, a gully offering an obvious way through. They could see the two dust columns converging on them, one behind and one to their left. The cops were gaining on them.

Jaxon rolled down the window.

"What are you doing?" Winston asked as she clambered over him.

"Getting on the roof. If I know Grunt, he'll have set up an ambush in that gully. We don't want to get shot by our own side."

Winston grabbed her ankle as she got halfway out of the window. "Wait! It's too dangerous!"

"It's only dangerous if you make me fall. Hands off!" Jaxon gave him a kick, not hard enough to hurt but hard enough to show she meant business. The Englishman let go.

Wind and sand blew in her face, nearly blinding

her. Luckily, the Land Rover had a heavy-duty luggage rack on top that gave her something sturdy to hang on to.

She needed it. The gully was rough with stones that had eroded down from the slopes on either side. Suddenly, she found herself bucking and jumping like some cowgirl breaking a stallion. An especially big rock made the Land Rover leap into the air, only to come down with a jarring crash. Jaxon did a face plant against the roof and almost lost her grip.

Still, she clung on, blinking blood out of her eyes. A shadow out of the corner of her eye made her look up the side of the gully. Sure enough, there knelt Grunt, rifle in hand, staring down at her in astonishment. Then he looked past her and spotted the dust column kicked up by the pursuit vehicles.

Jaxon didn't see any more after that. The way got even rougher, and it was all she could do to hang on. Mateo slowed down, but the ride still gave her several more bruises and nearly threw her off more than once.

Finally, the Land Rover broke free to the other side. The two Land Rovers of the Atlantis Allegiance stood parked half a kilometer away. Grunt came down the near slope and started sprinting for them.

Now that she had a smooth ride once again,

Jaxon could shift position and stick her head back in the window.

"Get back in here!" one of the Atlanteans shouted. She wasn't sure which one. Maybe it had been all of them.

"Go over and pick him up!" she shouted to Mateo.

The Peruvian grumbled something she couldn't hear, the wind whipping the words away, but he did as she told him.

Grunt took the hint, slung his rifle on his back, and angled toward the Land Rover.

"Slow down!" Jaxon shouted to Mateo. "You're going too fast!"

Mateo had only slowed down to about thirty miles an hour. That turned out not to be too fast for Grunt. He leaped into the air and grabbed the luggage rack. The pull of the vehicle made his body go horizontal, but he used that to his advantage and swung himself onto the top. Within a second, he was securely braced, and Mateo picked up speed.

"Nicely done," Jaxon said.

"Since when do you ride on the outside of cars?" the mercenary asked.

"Since half the Timbuktu police force got on our tail."

"Oh great, another typical day." Grunt peered through the windshield. Elaine waved at him. Mateo frowned.

"Atlanteans? These guys don't look local, though."

"No time to explain," Jaxon said. "We need to get out of here first."

Mateo screeched to a halt next to the two Land Rovers of the Atlantis Allegiance, enveloping Jaxon's friends in a cloud of sand. Jaxon and Grunt jumped off and hurried over to them.

"These are some Atlanteans here to help," Jaxon said. "The cops are about to come through that gully. Time to leave."

Dr. Yamazaki peered at the newcomers. "Are they from the same group that healed me?"

"Yes," Jaxon said, looking over her shoulder. A cloud of dust was just appearing in the gully. "Let's go."

They all hopped into the vehicles and peeled off across the desert. While they still had a lead on the police, their vehicles were no faster, and the cops tailed them until darkness ended the chase. At last, the Atlantis Allegiance and the Atlantis Guard made camp in a quiet area of sand dunes. Jaxon had no doubt the pursuit would resume the next day.

CHAPTER 2

AUGUST 17, 2016, THE DESERT FORTY-FIVE MILES NORTHEAST OF TIMBUKTU, MALI

11:00 P.M.

They didn't dare light a fire that night, so they ate a cold dinner under the starlight. Like always, the desert night sky was clear and brilliant with stars. The Milky Way arched overhead, billions of distant suns creating a band of illumination. Closer stars stood out as bright pinpricks of light. Jaxon found herself staring up at them, thinking how peaceful it all seemed.

Certainly more peaceful than their dinner.

The Atlantis Guard was reluctant to join in the

conversation, only answering questions in curt replies while ignoring any overtures of friendship from the Atlantis Allegiance. Mateo was openly rude.

They sat in a wide circle, the humans on one side, the Atlanteans on the other. All except for Jaxon, who sat between Otto and Vivian. In the dark, it was difficult to read the Atlanteans' expressions, but their attitude was clear enough.

Hostility and distrust. Even the most pleasant of the Atlanteans, Winston and Elaine, showed hostility and distrust.

Jaxon couldn't help but feel a bit of the same. She kept looking at Grunt and Vivian, trying to see them as friends. Back at the Russian hideout, they had gunned down Brett. Of course, he had been attacking her, trying to kill her. He had developed the strength and speed of an Atlantean, and despite her own powers, she had been losing that fight. Grunt and Vivian had saved her life.

And yet every time she looked at them, all she could see was a pair of murderers.

Stop, she told herself. *They did it to save you. They had no other choice.*

What a dirty world those two live in. No matter how good your side is, no matter how honorable you

try to be, innocent people always end up getting hurt.
No wonder they quit the Special Forces.

Jaxon slumped her shoulders. Now she lived in that same world. Her boyfriend, Otto Heike, rubbed her shoulders, but he obviously felt some tension of his own. He and Yuhle kept giving each other uncomfortable glances. They'd been prisoners of the Russians together. What had happened between them?

After an hour of failed small talk, Jaxon decided it was time to get down to business.

"So first things first. We need to avoid the cops tomorrow. Then we have to deal with Isadore. She was obviously sent by General Meade. Those twins who attacked Grunt with straight razors in Marrakech were probably from him as well. Now we just need to know why the Russians are mixed up in all this."

Yuhle adjusted the wreckage of his eyeglasses. They were bound together with a mixture of duct tape and wire. One lens had a chip out of the side and a hairline crack down the middle. "I think I can answer that." He paused and glanced at the Atlanteans.

"We can trust them," Jaxon said.

Grunt cocked his head. "I'm not sure we should—"

"We can trust them," Jaxon snapped. Otto's hand pulled away from her back. In a calmer voice, she continued. "They saved my life and saved Dr. Yamazaki's life. They're on our side, and we need all the help we can get."

Yuhle glanced at Yamazaki, who nodded. He took a deep breath and continued.

"When we were doing research in the manuscript museum, Dimitri and I discovered an old text talking about the healing water, recounting the same legend we heard before about it being the original water on Earth before the Flood. He'd seen one or two texts like this before, but this one was special. It gave the location."

"I remember you telling me this," Otto said. "It's here in Mali, isn't it?"

"Yes, by the ruins of an old caravanserai in the far north of the country. Part of the trading route through the desert to get to the wealthier nations like Morocco and Tunisia up north by the Mediterranean."

"Do you remember the name?" Jaxon asked.

"Sebil Baraka."

"That means 'blessed fountain' in Arabic," Grunt said and nodded. "Sounds like the place."

"So that's what the Russians are looking for," Jaxon said.

Yuhle adjusted his glasses. "Yes. Dimitri isn't really a historian. Well, he is, but not for purely academic reasons. It seems that while the United States government, or at least a rogue part of it, wants to control the Atlanteans, the Russians want to control this water."

"Damn," Grunt said. "It's like the Cold War all over again."

"Their genetic research is well behind ours," Dr. Yamazaki said, "but they have some of the best chemists in the world. Assuming they know about Project Poseidon at all, they probably figure the best way get ahead of the United States is to locate some sources of that water in order to analyze and replicate it. We didn't know a thing about that water in Project Poseidon, and I bet the Russians know we don't know. So yes, this is a case of two superpowers fighting for supremacy, just like in the days of the Soviet Union."

"With my people stuck in the middle," Jaxon said and sighed.

"I've been doing some checking," Vivian said.

"There are a lot of Russian archaeological teams in Mali and Mauritania, making surveys of the ancient sites. It's a perfect cover for spying."

"I guess those heavies we fought back in Timbuktu, the ones who came as reinforcements for Dimitri and Nadya, must have been some of those fake archaeologists," Otto said. "I'm surprised these countries would let them in. Wouldn't the government be suspicious of their motives?"

Vivian shrugged. "A bit of military aid and a few gold Rolexes for the generals go a long way here."

"So what do we do?" Jaxon asked, looking at Grunt and Vivian. They were the soldiers of the group.

"We go after the Russians first," Grunt said.

"But my people in Mauritania are stuck in a concentration camp in the desert!" Jaxon objected.

"What? What's this?" Mateo demanded.

"You haven't heard?" Jaxon said. "The Mauritanian government, probably prompted by the US, has rounded up all the Atlanteans."

"We have to get them out," Mateo said.

"I know, and we'll get them out as soon as we can," Grunt said. "But the Russians will be heading to that caravanserai immediately. It won't take long for Dimitri to find out where it is. With all his background in Malian history, he might know already. We can't let them get the water. If they do, it's all over."

"It's all over for my people if we don't get them out of that camp," Mateo said.

"They don't want to kill them," Dr. Yamazaki said. "They want to use them as test subjects."

"Oh, that makes it fine, then," Mateo sneered.

"No, it doesn't," Yamazaki said. "But it does give us some time. We don't have time when it comes to the Russians."

Elaine put a hand on Matco's shoulder. "They're right. Breaking them out of that camp will take some planning anyway. We have to go for this well first. The water will help us on our mission."

"But we don't know where this Sebil Baraka is!" Otto said.

"I know who might know," Jaxon said. "Daouda Ndiaye, the griot back in Timbuktu. He's like a walking encyclopedia."

"Good plan," Otto said. "We'll sneak someone back there to ask him."

"It has to be me," Jaxon replied. "He won't trust anyone but an Atlantean."

But will they even trust me? she asked herself. *They're all blaming me for the police crackdown.*

Otto shook his head. "Too dangerous."

Jaxon frowned at him. "You're not my keeper. Besides, I've been in danger ever since those government agents back in America took notice of me. Daouda doesn't trust outsiders. Considering our history, who can blame him? It has to be me."

Vivian put a hand on her shoulder. "I wish I didn't agree with you, honey, but I don't see any other way."

"Let's do it," Jaxon said.

She sounded more confident than she felt. The last she had heard, Daouda had been hauled off to the police station for questioning. That had been a couple of days ago. Surely they had released him by now.

Then there was another problem. With the police on the lookout for her, how was she going to get into Timbuktu unseen?

▭

The next morning, Vivian produced an answer to that.

She came up to Jaxon with a voluminous blue cloth over her arm.

"I brought this along in case we needed a disguise, honey."

She held it up. It looked like an upside-down cloth bag. At the closed end was a mesh screen.

"It's a burka," Jaxon said. She'd seen them on the news but never in real life.

"It's not used much around here. The conservative Muslim women wear niqabs. Those cover the face but leave a slit over the eyes open. Unfortunately, that means everyone will see your skin and eye color. So we have to go for the burka. Sadly, they're not unknown in this part of the world. More and more men are embracing strict Islam and forcing their women to wear them."

"I'm not anyone's woman. No man owns me."

"Lucky you."

"I'm not wearing that. It's like a flag for misogyny."

Vivian made a face. "I agree, honey, but would you rather spend a night alone in the police station? You might learn a lot more about misogyny than you ever wanted to."

Jaxon groaned. Vivian was right. When it came to tactical stuff, she always was.

"Give me that damn thing."

After five minutes wearing the burka, Jaxon wanted to faint. The Sahara was stifling enough in the middle of summer, but with a heavy cloth draped over you from the top of your head all the way down to your ankles, it felt as though someone had turned up the temperature twenty more degrees. Sweat poured down her, and she found herself breathing harder and faster just to suck enough air through that cloth mesh. That heated up the inside of the burka even more.

And she could barely see! The mesh made everything darker and indistinct, like wearing a pair of badly scratched sunglasses.

After she had walked around for a few minutes to try to accustom herself to it, she went back to the assembled group.

If Otto laughs, I'm going to slug him, she promised herself.

But Otto didn't laugh. Instead he looked grim and a bit embarrassed.

"I hate this thing," Jaxon declared.

"So do I," Vivian said, "but it served me well in Pakistan."

"Isn't this just going to attract more attention to me? I've never seen anyone wearing one of these around here."

"They do in some of the more remote villages,

thanks to foreign preachers coming in," Grunt said. "The rich oil countries are spending a lot of money trying to convert the rest of the Muslim world into their strict brand of Islam."

"Wonderful."

Otto shook his head. "It's ... horrible. But it will get you through town and to the griot's house without anyone recognizing you."

"Great," Jaxon said, letting out a great gust of air. "Now I just need to convince them to talk to me."

With the help of Elaine's drone, they avoided the police and approached Timbuktu along a little-used track through the desert.

Since they couldn't risk driving into the city, they dropped Jaxon off at a village by the lone paved highway to wait for a bus. She sat under the ragged tarpaulin stretched between wooden stakes that served as the bus stop, trying not to faint from the heat. She kept looking around, worried that she stuck out.

She did. Men gave her sidelong glances and moved farther away. The women looked at her either curiously or with expressions of open disdain. Thankfully, none talked to her. Otherwise, she'd have had a tough time explaining why she was dressed like this and not able to speak Arabic.

In fact, no one spoke with her at all. It didn't look as if anyone wanted to.

She got on the bus, handing the driver exact change so she didn't have to say anything, and sat near the back. The drive was a long one, with the bus stopping every kilometer or so to take on or let off an endless stream of passengers. The heat made her queasy and drowsy, and she felt as if she would fall asleep if it weren't for her nerves. She wasn't sure she could pull this off.

At last, the bus parked in Timbuktu central bus station, which was nothing more than an open square in front of the main mosque crowded with battered old buses. She stumbled off the bus, half-unconscious. Now she knew why men made their female relations wear these things—it kept them inside the house. No one could go out and about and have a normal life wearing a burka. She couldn't even see properly. The grand mosque with its towering sloped walls of brown adobe topped by tall minarets usually looked grand in the sun. Now it looked hazy and bland. The whole world looked hazy and bland through this thing.

Jaxon staggered more than walked to Daouda Ndiaye's house. As far as she could see through the mesh cloth screen that covered her face, the police she passed barely looked at her. The burka had made her invisible.

But I don't want to be invisible, Jaxon thought. *At least not in normal life.*

But when do I get a normal life again?

She tried to think back to when her life was normal and couldn't. She'd always been an outcast, an unwanted ward of the state. At least she had a place now. She had fellow Atlanteans and her friends in the Atlantis Allegiance to rely on. But why did that have to come at the price of risking her life?

Quit whining and do the mission. Grunt had said that to Otto once. It sounded like good advice. She wished doing this mission didn't have to be so hot, though.

And smelly. She was getting funky inside this thing.

At last, she made it to the griot's home, passing along a street that she knew was mostly made up of Atlantean homes. That street was deserted. Where children usually played and adults sold their wares from open market stalls, now she saw only closed doors and shuttered windows.

She pounded on Daouda's door. After a long pause, with Jaxon roasting in the sun, there came a suspicious voice in Arabic. It sounded like Hawa, the griot's daughter. She was a teacher and could speak English.

"Hawa, it's me!"

There was another long pause. Jaxon thought she heard whispered conversation on the other side of the door.

Suddenly, the door burst open. Hawa did a double take when she saw the burka, glanced both ways along the street, and yanked her inside. Being Atlantean, she did it with enough force to take Jaxon off her feet.

"Ow!"

The door slammed shut behind her.

"What are you doing here?" Hawa demanded.

Jaxon pulled the burka off her. It stuck to her sweaty body, and she had to struggle for a moment.

"And why are you wearing that thing?" Hawa went on. "Now the police are going to think we are aligned with the Islamists."

"No police saw me come here."

"There are always eyes that see."

Jaxon stood there panting. Her shirt was stuck to her body, soaked in sweat. Hawa's frown softened.

"Come to the sitting room. I'll get you some water."

Jaxon slumped on the cushioned floor.

After a minute, Hawa returned with a glass and a large pitcher of water. She let Jaxon drain two full glasses before she asked, "Why did you come here? You are endangering all of us."

"I'm sorry. We didn't want to mess things up for you. I just need to know one thing, and I will go."

"What?"

"Dimitri is a spy for the Russian government. He's been looking for sources of the original water, and he's found one at an old caravan rest stop called Sebil Baraka. He's a historian, and he'll know where that is. I need to find out, too, so we can stop him. If he takes the water for the Russians, who knows what bad purposes they'll use it for."

"Power," came Daouda Ndiaye's deep voice. "That is what they all want."

The old griot limped into the sitting room. The side of his face was swollen, and he favored one leg. Hawa rushed to help him and eased him down onto the cushions. Jaxon stared, her stomach turning.

"The police beat you up!"

"Asking me questions I could not answer," Daouda said as Hawa set more cushions around him. "And wouldn't even if I could."

"I can't believe it. They'll pay for this!"

Daouda raised a calming hand. "There is no

point getting angry at the ignorant. There are too many, and it will give you heart trouble. Now what were you saying about Dimitri? I never did trust that man."

Jaxon explained all that had transpired since she had last seen him, leaving nothing out. She sobbed as she told of Brett appearing, and how he had been used as a guinea pig by a rogue faction of the US government.

Daouda and Hawa listened in grim silence. When Jaxon finished, they sat thinking for a minute. Jaxon took the opportunity to drink another glass of water. At last, the griot spoke.

"I have never heard of Sebil Baraka, but I know where I can look it up. Hawa, get me box number 23, please."

Jaxon smiled. The griot had a room full of boxes containing old manuscripts. While many families had given up their treasured heirlooms to the manuscript museum, some scholars such as Daouda had kept them. They had, however, accepted the museum's gift of acid-free sealable boxes they could use to better preserve their treasures.

Hawa returned with a heavy box about twice the size of a shoebox. She set it beside her father, who opened it and rifled through its contents. At last, he brought out a yellowed manuscript. The binding had long since disappeared, and worms had eaten holes through a couple of pages. Before the museum had been set up, Jaxon had been told, the local people didn't know anything about preserving manuscripts and often kept them in bad conditions, such as inside folders of modern bleached paper that leached acid onto the fragile pages.

Daouda slowly flipped through the pages, carefully setting each one aside as he finished with it. Every now and then, he stopped, his eyebrows going up with surprise, or he made a little satisfied hum to himself when he read something especially interesting.

Jaxon watched with increasing impatience. With the cops looking for her and her friends in danger outside of town, watching someone do research was just about the most agonizing thing imaginable. She could never be a scholar.

At last, he finished.

"Ah yes, here it is. Sebil Baraka, the next caravanserai north of Teroudant."

"And where's Teroudant?"

"It has changed its name over the years. Since the caravan route disappeared and was replaced with a truck route on a different path, it has shrunk from a major trading town to a little village called Sheikh ibn Tulun. There's an interesting story about how and why the name changed. You see, ibn Tulun was a ruler in Egypt—"

"Please, my friends are waiting for me."

"Oh, very well. If you take the northern road out of Timbuktu, after about two hundred kilometers, you will come to the village of Araouane. From there, you go another fifty kilometers to the northwest to Sheikh ibn Tulun. There's not much there these days. Then you go another twenty miles northwest to Sebil Baraka. It's not on any maps, so you might have trouble finding it."

"I won't have any trouble. The last well I found, in Mauritania, I found just by sensing it. I even tested that ability by going back. If we get within twenty or thirty kilometers of the place, I'll be able to lead the team right to it."

Daouda and Hawa looked at each other and then back at her.

"Remember that prophecy I mentioned?" Daouda said. "Of a lost child returning and saving her people? It mentioned that the child could sense the original water."

"Yeah, I remember. It also mentioned that she'd

be rejected by her people and they'd never appreciate what she did for them."

They stared at each other for a moment in silence. When Daouda spoke, his voice was heavy with resignation.

"God has written our fates, and we can only play our part. Good luck on your journey."

Jaxon hugged them. "I'm going to need it."

CHAPTER 3

AUGUST 19, 2016, HEADQUARTERS OF THE POSEIDON PROJECT, ALBUQUERQUE, NEW MEXICO
11:45 A.M.

General Arnold Corbin sat in the laboratory of the Poseidon Project and watched Dr. Jones put the two Atlanteans through their paces. Well, one and a half Atlanteans. Orion was a pureblood Atlantean they had kidnapped. General Meade was an artificial Atlantean made by a special serum, just like that Brett Lawson kid. Pity he'd been killed by the Atlantis Allegiance before they had gotten a chance to run more tests on him, but the serum was relatively cheap to make, and they could make as many foot soldiers as they wanted to.

But the serum had drawbacks. It had dulled Meade's intellect, made him a psychological slave. That was a poor trait in a soldier. A soldier needed to take orders, yes, but he also had to think for himself, solve problems. Ziegler, a professional hypnotist, had been busy giving Meade the ability to think independently. Ziegler had made great strides, but Meade's cognitive abilities were still nothing compared to what they had been.

And the hypnotic conditioning they'd put Orion through didn't leave him much better off. It would be some time before they could operate independently.

But what physical traits! General Meade was bench-pressing three hundred pounds now. No normal middle-aged man, no matter how fit, could do that. Orion could bench five hundred pounds. Plus, they both could run more than twenty miles an hour and keep up that pace for an entire morning.

Yes, it was all coming together. A few more months, and he'd be ready to strike. Soon, he'd be dictator of the United States, and he'd put this corrupt, lazy country back on its feet.

General Corbin had done his homework. He knew

that every dictator needed three things to gain power—
an external threat, an army loyal only to him, and chaos
in the civilian government. The army was coming along
nicely, although not nearly as quickly as Corbin would
have liked. The external threat was being provided by a
team of photo and video forgers who were busy putting
ominous reports of alien abductions and UFO sightings
into the world's media, and even into the top-secret files
of the US government. Meade had fallen for it, and
other members of the military and many members of
the civilian government were quietly concerned that all
these UFO reports might actually pose a real threat.

A large portion of the public, of course, had swallowed the bait hook, line, and sinker. But then the
public would swallow anything. Jaded, pathetic, and
poorly educated with no capacity for critical thinking, they needed a dictatorship.

As for chaos in the civilian government, that was
coming along nicely too. His team of hackers, forgers,
and bloggers at Operation Bicker fed the public a
relentless diet of fake news. He'd managed to wreck
the campaigns of two major presidential candidates,
one for each party, so now both parties were scram-
bling to find replacements. Corbin's connections had
provided him with the list of candidates that each
party had drawn up, and his team was already plan-

ning to take every one of them down. Mistresses, racist comments, drunk driving—whatever seemed the most appropriate. The folks at Operation Bicker were creative geniuses.

Of course, there was pushback to all this. Some of the smarter TV pundits complained about so many of the scandals turning out to be false, but it didn't matter, because most of the time, the public had such a short attention span that they only remembered the original story, not the correction or retraction that came along a week later. The original tale was always more attractive and juicy anyway.

The old saying went: "You can fool some of the people all of the time, and all of the people some of the time, but you can't fool all of the people all of the time."

He didn't need to. He just needed to get the public into a confused, bickering mess that couldn't separate fact from fiction. Polls showed that confidence in the government had plunged to an all-time low, and elements of the right were now openly admiring fascism. On the left, everyone was too busy condemning each other for not being sufficiently liberal to notice who their real enemies were.

But he still had some obstacles to overcome. The Atlantis Allegiance was a constant thorn in his side, and he still hadn't tracked down the shadowy group of Atlanteans who had saved Dr. Yamazaki and somehow healed her from her stroke. Now reports indicated that both groups were on the move in Mali.

Things were developing too fast in North Africa, and he was outnumbered over there.

Besides Isadore, the only boots he had on the ground right now were the McKay twins. A pair of psychopaths, but professional psychopaths who could be relied upon to get the job done. They had wounded and perhaps killed Grunt, and certainly put him out of commission for a long while. Now they were headed down to Timbuktu to take care of the rest of the Atlantis Allegiance.

General Corbin drummed his fingers on his desk. As deadly as those two were, he didn't think they'd be enough, not with Russian spies and perhaps an Atlantean group thrown into the mix. No, he needed to send reinforcements.

He called Dr. Jones over to him.

"They seem to be doing well. How's the progress with their mental state?" he snapped. General Corbin wasn't one to waste words.

"Good. Their cognitive abilities have grown substantially."

"Enough that they can go on a mission of their own?"

"No, sir."

"And the new arrivals?"

His operatives had just lured six teenage runaways off the streets.

"The serum is working well on five of them. Unfortunately, one had a weak heart, and the serum proved too much for his system. He had a heart attack. We managed to revive him, but he's going to need—"

"Get rid of him. There's no room for weaklings in this world."

The scientist's face turned grim. Corbin glared at him.

At last Dr. Jones replied, "Yes, sir."

"Besides their cognitive abilities, are Meade and Orion ready to take on a mission?"

"Yes, sir. The five teenagers probably won't be ready for at least another month."

General Corbin slammed his fist on the desk. "We can't wait that long. Get Meade and Orion prepped. They're flying out tomorrow."

"Who's going to lead them, sir? I need to stay here and oversee the new subjects."

"I'm leading them. It's time to take out the Atlantis Allegiance once and for all."

―――

Isadore Grant watched as the identical twins approached down the dusty street of Goundam, a town about a hundred kilometers west of Timbuktu. They looked even more out of place than she did. Not many outsiders came to this little town of about sixteen thousand people. There were no big factories or any other industry to attract foreigners and nothing to see besides the main mosque, which a Western woman like her would never be allowed to enter. The only plus to this hick town was that it had a little airport with flights from Bamako, Mali's capital. The McKay twins had been able to avoid Timbuktu, which was now on high alert.

She frowned as she saw every head turn as they passed. Heads turned for her, too, but at least she dressed unobtrusively, in loose khaki pants and shirt and a headscarf. Those two stuck out like sore thumbs.

They had stocky bodies and thick, dispropor-
tionate arms that reminded her of gorillas. Both were

identically dressed in black dress shoes, black pants, and buttoned-up white dress shirts.

Isadore shook her head. Granted, a Westerner could never blend in with the locals in a place like this, but they looked as though they had just stepped through a teleporter from Hackney in east London.

She'd heard this was these guys' trademark. They never wore a disguise on the job like most assassins, and if at all possible, they took out their targets with straight razors. Not the most efficient method, but it did give them a hell of a reputation in the business.

They walked right for her, not needing to be told that she was their contact. She was the only foreigner in the whole place.

They stopped in front of her. She tried to put on a brave face. The things she'd been told about these two made her skin crawl.

"I'm Ronnie," one said in a Cockney accent.

"I'm Reggie," the other said in an identical tone. Isadore couldn't tell them apart. It didn't matter—they were a unit.

"I'm Isadore Grant."

"We know. Let's get to it."

"Follow me," Isadore said. She almost asked how their flight had been but decided against it. They didn't look like the kind of people who engaged in small talk.

She had a 4x4 parked at the edge of town. It wasn't as good as a Land Rover for navigating the tracks that passed for roads in this part of the world, but it was the best she could steal on a moment's notice. They climbed in the back seat, and Isadore drove out into the desert. They could steal a better vehicle later.

"You flew, so I suppose you don't have any guns," Isadore said. "Look under your seats, and you'll find a pair of 9mm automatics, courtesy of some Russians I bumped off. I'll tell you about them in a minute."

The twins reached under their seats and retrieved the weapons as well as some spare clips of ammunition.

"What other weapons do you have?" one of them asked. She couldn't tell if it was Ronnie or Reggie.

"A pair of Kalashnikovs with plenty of ammo and a selection of poisons."

Those came courtesy of Stephen, her husband, one of the world's leading experts in toxins. She decided not to share that bit of information with the McKay twins. The less they knew about her, the better.

"Where are we going?" one of them asked.

"I don't know yet," Isadore admitted.

The twins took this news with silence. She glanced at them in the rearview mirror. They sat with their hands on their legs, staring straight ahead.

As she drove out of town, Isadore added, "Grunt showed up here the other day. You guys cut him up really badly, but he still had some fight in him."

"I got him in the gut," one of the twins said. "He'll die of internal bleeding soon enough."

"Don't count on it."

Grunt was a hard man to put down. She'd seen him take plenty of punishment and still finish the mission. He had looked pretty bad, though, and had probably run out of gas after that fight. If he went to a hospital, at least he'd be out of the picture for a while.

Isadore was surprised to notice she felt a faint glimmer of hope that he did survive. He had been a fun boyfriend, a bit too softhearted but in many ways more her kind of man than her husband.

She shook that thought off as unworthy. She and Stephen made a great team. That man knew how to make some serious money, and working together, they were going to make a fortune. That was all that mattered. She thought back on all the dilapidated farmhouses she had lived in, all the trailer parks, all the ramen and the cold leftover beans she had to eat instead of real food. Grunt could never have given her the kind of life she deserved. A man like him would never align himself with the likes of General Corbin. Too many principles.

Isadore snorted. Principles were for victims. No one got to be a billionaire by sticking to principles. And Corbin had promised them billions.

Once she got out of sight of the last building, she slowed down and went off road for a kilometer then stopped.

"Time to find out where we're going," she said.

She got out and opened up the trunk. Inside was a hulky Russian man, obviously military but with a most unmilitary look of abject terror on his face. Duct tape covered his mouth, and his hands were tied behind his back with thick cords. Both his kneecaps had been broken with a hammer. Isadore knew just where to hit.

"Do you speak Russian?" she asked the McKay twins, who stared at the prisoner with stony faces.

"No."

"It doesn't matter. I do. I'll take care of the questions while you make him answer."

"Righto."

They grabbed him and pulled him out.

Isadore got up close to the Russian's face and said in his own language, "My companions here are homicidal maniacs." The prisoner's eyes went wide as a pair of straight razors shone in the desert sun. "They are going to give you a little sample of their work. After a minute or two, I'll make them stop. Then you are going to tell me everything about your mission. If I'm convinced you've told me everything, I'll shoot you in the head. If not, I'll let them work some more."

It only took five minutes for Isadore to learn everything.

CHAPTER 4

AUGUST 19, THE DESERT NORTH OF
TIMBUKTU, MALI
10:00 A.M.

"If anyone would like to know," Yuhle announced,
"it is currently 42.8 degrees centigrade outside."

"What's that in English?" Otto asked.

"The English use the metric system. As do scientists. It's more precise. In fact, only the general population of the United States still uses Imperial
measurements. Ironically, that measurement system
was invented by the English, who gave it up in favor
of the metric system invented by the French."

"Whatever," Otto groaned. "Could you please
translate?"

"It's 109 degrees Fahrenheit."

Otto groaned again. "Why can't all these lost cities be in the Bahamas or something?"

"I better not have to put on that burka again," Jaxon grumbled.

"It wasn't flattering," Otto said.

"You don't know the half of it."

Jaxon looked out the window, her mind still in turmoil. The reappearance and sudden death of Brett was a constant background ache. It felt profoundly unfair to lose him a second time. Then there was the rage at the shadowy figures who turned him into some freak and got him killed, and the fear of knowing that those same figures were after her in order to do far worse. If this mission didn't succeed, if this long shot didn't land a bull's-eye, she would end up a lab rat somewhere.

She looked out at the rolling dunes as they sped along a barren track. They were alone except for the Land Rover of Atlanteans a hundred meters or so ahead of them. They hadn't seen a police or army patrol all day, hadn't even seen another vehicle for hours. This desert seemed to stretch forever.

The vastness of it, the emptiness, lulled her. At first when she got here, she hated the desert. It scared her, all that empty, deadly space. Now it made her feel something close to peace. There was purity to it, honesty. And the people here had purity and honesty, too, at least most of them. Now she understood why so many adventurers felt attached to the desert. She remembered one of her foster fathers had made her watch *Lawrence of Arabia*. It was a total guy movie. She suspected that particular foster father had wanted to foster a boy, because he was always trying to get her to play football and watch war movies. This movie had actually been pretty good, though. The shots of the Arabian Desert had been beautiful, and one line had stuck with her. Someone had asked Lawrence why an Englishman would love the desert, and he replied, "It is clean."

And it was.

It was the only place where she had ever felt at peace, first when she had been hiding out in the Sonoran Desert in Arizona, and now here in the Sahara. It didn't matter that she'd been hunted in the desert by trained killers, or that the desert itself had nearly made her die a slow, excruciating death of thirst. There was simplicity here that appealed to her. Every time she lived in a city, everything got all messed up, and most of the time, it was her fault. Los Angeles had been a disaster. So had Marrakech. So had Timbuktu. She kept leaving messes behind her.

And now she had to go out across the endless desert to fix them.

The walkie-talkie crackling woke her up from her reverie. Dr. Yamazaki's voice came over the airwaves. She was driving the lead vehicle.

"Araouane is just up ahead. I can just see it. Two options. The track passes right through it. We can pass through and stop to top off our gas tanks, or we can make a detour through the desert."

Grunt picked up the walkie-talkie lying on the dashboard.

"If they're going to hit us, they'll do it away from civilization. We could use the extra gas for more maneuverability. Once we get to Sebil Baraka, we might have to wait for the Russkies for a while, and we might have to get out of there quick and set out across the desert."

There was a pause, then Dr. Yamazaki replied, "Agreed."

"Agreed," came Trisha's voice from the other Land Rover. "That place the griot mentioned called Sheikh ibn Tulun isn't even on the map. So I guess this is the last outpost of civilization."

Araouane certainly looked the part. Situated in a little bowl of a valley amid bleak sand dunes, it was a cluster of about fifty squat concrete buildings. They all looked identical except for a whitewashed little mosque that shone so brightly in the sun it hurt to look at it.

They drove through the cluster of buildings set every which way with no real streets between them, just open dusty space, found the gas station, and parked in front of the gas pumps. The station was a larger building that also had a mechanics shop. Atop it stood a tall radio antenna. Yuhle looked at it suspiciously.

"What if the local police take notice of us and radio back to Timbuktu?" the geneticist asked.

"In this dump, there probably aren't any local police," Otto said.

"There are always local police, honey," Vivian said. "But one of those Atlanteans said he could take care of it."

"Which one? Winston?" Jaxon asked.

"Is that the British guy?"

"Yes."

"That's the one."

Jaxon grinned. "Then I think we'll be all right. Just sit back and watch some Atlantean magic."

"There's no such thing as magic," Dr. Yamazaki said.

"Then explain what happens next."

Already, a few people had begun to gather. Jaxon suspected that vehicles pulling up at the gas station was the only type of entertainment they got here. And when those vehicles were full of Westerners and People of the Sea, it was like a New Year's Eve party.

The novelty of seeing so many strange faces didn't make the locals forget the reason for their town's existence, however. Several men, women, and children hurried over with baskets filled with water bottles and packets of biscuits. While nobody really needed any more supplies, several people, Jaxon included, bought a few things just to be friendly. This place was the only inhabited spot worth stopping in for a hundred miles in either direction, and if it weren't for the faint track through the desert that the occasional truck passed along, it would cease to exist.

Trisha used her Arabic to get some gas, and they had barely started to fill up the tanks when a couple of cops broke through the circle of onlookers. Everybody in the Atlantis Allegiance tensed.

"I hope you speak Arabic, too, Winston, because you're going to need it," Jaxon whispered.

The Englishman only smiled. "I communicate in a different way."

The two policemen carried AK-47s like most of their compatriots, and they looked at the newcomers with open suspicion. Winston walked up to them, holding out a pack of cigarettes.

One of the policemen barked out a question.

"Would you like a cigarette?" Winston said in a friendly, soothing voice. "Of course you would. Both of you would. A nice, relaxing cigarette. Nothing like a good smoke, eh? Here you go."

The two cops stared at the packet of cigarettes, which Winston waved back and forth in a slow, steady motion.

"Here you go. It's all right. Have a smoke."

The cops' eyes hooded. They each took a cigarette. Winston lighted them, and the two officers sauntered away. The crowd looked on in confusion.

"Well, I'll be damned," Grunt said. "You should work for the tobacco industry."

"A vile habit. I only carry cigarettes because they make a good prop. Half the people here probably think I slipped them some money."

As they finished filling up, Jaxon looked around her. From where she stood, she could see half the town, all ugly concrete buildings that looked more like bunkers than homes. Beyond lay only sand dunes. Then she looked at the people, aged early by the harsh desert yet bearing themselves with pride.

"You know, we have it really easy in the States," Jaxon said.

Otto nodded. "Yeah, I was thinking the same thing."

Once they filled the tanks, they didn't waste any time. Within a minute, they had passed the last of the houses and were back in the open desert. Araouane vanished as if it never existed.

"I talked with a couple of the locals," Trisha said over the walkie-talkie. "They haven't seen any other foreigners in months."

"So we're ahead of the Russians," Otto said. "That's a relief."

"Either that, or they went around Araouane and are ahead of us," Grunt said.

Grunt was proven right just a few miles farther on.

Jaxon saw the attack a second before it happened.

There was a glint of sunlight on metal from a flat, open area to their right. An instant later, there was a red flash. A blur cut across their front and slammed into the Atlantean Land Rover at the head of their column. The Land Rover exploded, flying to the left and overturning. Jaxon screamed.

Grunt yanked on the wheel and swerved to the right. A couple of bullets thunked into the vehicle. Jaxon couldn't see where they came from. As Yuhle and Otto hunkered down on the floor, Jaxon looked behind them to see what was happening with Dr. Yamazaki and Vivian. Their Land Rover swerved, too, Dr. Yamazaki expertly cutting off the track and heading for the cover of some dunes half a kilometer to their right. But they couldn't outrun the ambush. Jaxon looked desperately at them as she saw a line of bullet holes suddenly appear on the side of the vehicle. Dr. Yamazaki seemed to lose control. The Land Rover moved erratically, beginning to slow.

Another flash and another blur. It roared right past them and exploded a few meters in front of Dr. Yamazaki and Vivian's Land Rover. The shock wave made the vehicle lurch and grind to a halt.

Grunt slammed on the gas and sped away.

"Wait!" Jaxon cried. "We have to go back and get them!"

"We have to save ourselves and take out that Russian with the rocket-propelled grenade first," Grunt said, making for a cluster of boulders not far ahead. Bullets spat up plumes of sand all around them.

Grunt screeched to a halt just behind the rocks, which were big enough to hide the Land Rover from view. He grabbed his sniper's rifle and leaped out of the Land Rover. Otto came right behind him with an AK-47. Within a second, they had taken up positions on the rock, firing away at the unseen enemy. As Yuhle tried to get their companions on the radio, Jaxon grabbed a pair of binoculars to watch the fight.

First, she trained them on the two Land Rovers. The one owned by the Atlantis Guard lay on its side, smoking. She could see no one around it. When she turned to look at the one with Dr. Yamazaki and Vivian, she saw it parked with its doors open while a dark silhouetted figure dragged another figure away.

The crack of a bullet hitting the rock near her made her duck. She had barely heard it over the roar of Otto's AK-47 and the steady fire of Grunt's sniper's rifle. How many other bullets had come close that she hadn't heard?

The gunfire died down as Otto ran out of ammunition. Cursing, he fumbled to get the magazine out and replace it with a fresh one.

"Save your ammo, pyro," Grunt said. He paused

to take another shot then added, "Switch to single shots. Full auto at this range won't hit a damn thing."

Jaxon moved to a narrow fissure between two rocks and peeked through with the binoculars just in time to see another flash.

"Incoming!" Grunt shouted. Jaxon and Otto hit the dirt.

Grunt did not. He took another shot an instant before the rocket-propelled grenade hit. The explosion jabbed into Jaxon's ears. She watched in horror as Grunt flew backward to land on his back a few feet away.

"No!" Otto shouted, leaping up and running to him.

Grunt lay slack in his arms. Tears ran down Otto's cheeks. "You can't die!"

Grunt opened his eyes. "Oh yes, I can, but not today."

The mercenary struggled to his feet and smacked Otto on the back of the head. "Quiet blubbering and get back into position."

Otto grinned, grabbed his gun, and hurried to do what he was told.

"Boys will be boys," Jaxon mumbled, returning to her spot with her binoculars.

She scanned the barren stretch of desert. A

couple of figures lay in the sand, not moving. Then she focused on where the RPG had been firing from. She saw the Russians had dug a narrow trench in the sand. It was hard to see even with the binoculars and would have been all but invisible to the casual glance while driving by. In fact, Jaxon had been looking right at it and didn't see a thing until just before the guy fired.

He wasn't firing now. He lay half out of the trench, sprawled in an unnatural position, his rocket launcher still gripped in his dead fingers. Jaxon shuddered.

Then she realized why Grunt hadn't taken cover. When the Russian exposed himself to fire, Grunt used the opportunity to shoot him at the risk of his own life.

Bang. Grunt's gun fired again. A distant figure pirouetted and fell. *Bang.* He continued firing with ruthless efficiency.

Jaxon turned back to look at Dr. Yamazaki and Vivian. For a panicked moment, she couldn't locate them, then she spotted the flare of a gun muzzle from behind a low dune. So it was Vivian who was okay and the geneticist who was hurt. More fire came from her position as Otto started firing again, and even Yuhle picked up a gun and joined in.

"How are you going to hit anything, wearing those broken glasses?" Grunt asked.

"More bullets going in their direction can't be a bad thing," Yuhle replied.

"Very scientific reasoning, Doc," Grunt said and laughed.

But the gunfight didn't last much longer. One by one, the Russians got picked off. With the expert shooting of the two mercenaries, they didn't have much of a chance. As far as Jaxon could tell, Otto and Yuhle just filled the air with pointless bullets. Not that she was going to complain. Her mind was too occupied with wondering how the others were faring.

As soon as Grunt called the all clear, she sprinted for Vivian and Dr. Yamazaki's position.

"You okay?" she called as she sped over to them. To her profound relief, she saw Dr. Yamazaki sitting on the sand, tying up a wound on her thigh. Her face was etched with pain, but the wound didn't look serious. Without slowing, Jaxon veered off and picked up speed, running for the overturned Land Rover.

What she saw there made her want to keep on running until she got a thousand miles away.

Mateo stood guard with a rifle while Elaine, bleeding from a nasty gash to her forehead, bent over

Winston. He was covered with blood, and one arm had nearly been severed from his body. Jaxon brought her hand to her mouth and backed up a step.

Elaine's face set in deep concentration. She laid her hands on Winston's arm and let out a long, slow, deep breath.

Then something remarkable happened. In front of her eyes, Jaxon saw the wound heal, the muscles and bones and ligaments knit back together, and the arm become whole again. Elaine passed her hands over a deep cut in Winston's side and then another along his thigh. Both of those healed up within a second.

Once she was done, Elaine let out a ragged cry and toppled over. Jaxon rushed to her.

"Are you all right?"

"It takes a lot out of me," Elaine whispered.

"Where's Trisha?" Jaxon asked, looking at the overturned Land Rover.

"Don't look in there," Mateo said.

Jaxon felt a queasy feeling in her stomach. "Is she..."

"There are wounds even I can't heal," Elaine whimpered.

"Dr. Yamazaki is injured," Jaxon said.

"She's too tired to heal anyone else," Mateo said.

Winston groaned and began to stir. Elaine struggled to her feet.

"Take me to her."

Jaxon picked her up and hurried over with her. Despite being her size, with Jaxon's strength, it took no more effort than a regular human carrying a large bag of groceries, and she ran as fast as an Olympic sprinter.

"Let me see that," Elaine said as Jaxon laid her down next to the geneticist.

The Atlantean took off the bandage.

"A clean wound. The bullet went right through and didn't hit the bone. This won't take much energy."

She pressed her hand against the wound. Yamazaki breathed a sigh of relief as the wound healed up.

Dr. Yamazaki smiled. "That's the second time you folks have healed me."

To Jaxon's surprise, Elaine gave her a hard look. "I'm doing this because you're out here trying to help. But we know all about Project Poseidon."

Dr. Yamazaki grew serious. "I didn't know General Meade would turn it to his own uses. Yuhle and I started it with the best of intentions."

Elaine snorted and sat down. She looked equal parts angry and exhausted.

"Humans and their good intentions," she muttered.

"Aren't you going to heal your own cut?" Jaxon asked.

Elaine gave a bitter smile. "It's a limitation to my power. I can't heal myself. Not sure why. I guess it's because I transfer my energy to the patient. That's why I feel so tired after healing. I guess can't use my own energy to heal my own wounds."

"Allow me," Dr. Yamazaki said, picking up the medical case she had used on herself.

Elaine didn't look at her as the geneticist cleaned the wound, daubed it with iodine, and put a large bandage on it.

Grunt and Yuhle came over.

"We have a healer in the group," Dr. Yamazaki told him. "But she can't heal herself, so protecting her is top priority."

"Protecting *Jaxon* is top priority," Elaine corrected her.

"Agreed," Grunt said. "Glad to have you on board, Elaine."

Elaine didn't look at him either.

Jaxon suddenly noticed Otto wasn't there. "Where's Otto?"

"Back by the rocks."

Jaxon hurried back to him. She wanted to double-check he was okay.

He wasn't. Jaxon found him bent double behind the Land Rover, throwing up his breakfast. Jaxon knelt down by him and rubbed his back.

"What happened?"

Otto didn't answer for a moment. His hands trembled.

"I ... I think I got one."

"What?"

"One of the Russians. I think I hit one."

"Oh, Otto."

She didn't know what to say beyond that. She had always teased him about emulating Grunt, always laughed about how he was so eager for target practice and swaggered around with his gun. He sure wasn't swaggering now.

"We had to do it," he said, spitting out the last of the bile. "It was them or us, right? That's how it's supposed to work. You're not supposed to feel bad afterward. I mean, he was trying to kill me. He was trying to kill you. And until you showed up, I was crying like a baby."

He started crying again. Jaxon hugged him.

"I bet Grunt feels bad afterward."

"Him? That guy is made of concrete," Otto sniffled.

"No, he isn't. He cares about you. And I know you care about him."

"I... I don't think I can face another firefight."

"No one's asking you to."

"Yeah, tell that to all the people trying to kill us."

Jaxon didn't have a response to that.

Mateo came over. "We have to get the gear together and get out of here. We may be in the middle of nowhere, but that doesn't mean nobody saw. And there may be more Russians on our tail."

Otto picked himself up. "Back to work." He sighed then looked at Jaxon. "Don't tell Grunt."

She put a hand on his shoulder. "I won't, but you should."

Otto shook his head. He put the guns in the Land Rover, and they drove over to the others.

They hurriedly assembled all their gear. Dr. Yamazaki changed a tire that had gotten shot out, and Grunt checked the two vehicles to make sure there was no other damage. Vivian went around the battlefield, retrieving any useful items from the dead Russians, and came back with the rocket-propelled grenade launcher and a load of other weapons. The Atlantis Guard recovered whatever gear they could salvage from the wreck of their own Land Rover and shifted it over to the other two vehicles.

"I saw the Land Rover take a direct hit," Jaxon said to Mateo. "I'm amazed that rocket didn't tear it apart."

"It's an armored one," he replied. "Reinforced-steel plates on the sides and ends, plus bulletproof glass. We bought it here. Good thing we did, or we'd all be dead."

The Atlanteans wrapped Trisha up in a blanket, dug a hurried grave, and put her inside. As everyone stood around it, heads bowed, Winston spoke.

"Trisha Alverson was a good woman and a strong fighter for our cause. Always generous, always welcoming, she raised two Atlantean orphans like they were her own children. Those children are now orphans once again. They will be taken care of by our community, but they will never get over this loss. Nor shall we. But we must move on. The freedom of our people is too important for us to lose our resolve when one of us falls. She will be remembered."

"She will be remembered," the Atlanteans said together.

"She will be remembered," Jaxon repeated.

Through the tears welling in her eyes, she could see a spreading bloodstain on the blanket.

The Atlantis Guard covered the grave up with sand, and in silence, they all crowded into the two remaining Land Rovers.

The rest of the route passed without incident. They skirted by the village of Sheikh ibn Tulun without stopping. It was a sand-swept cluster of tents and a few concrete buildings. A couple of acres of palm trees and some stubble of grass showed the few dozen villagers had a well. Jaxon was glad to see no radio tower. She couldn't imagine what it must be like to live in such isolation.

Boring but more peaceful than anything I've ever had, she mused.

"We should be getting close," Yuhle said, squinting at a topo map. "Your friend's description was vague, but the way the terrain is laid out here, the old trade route should have gone straight ahead. See how the land gets rough to either side? The best route is straight to the north."

Otto peered over his shoulder. He still looked pale. "That's a pretty wide area. Let's hope we can spot it."

"I'll find it," Jaxon said.

She sat back in her seat and didn't take part in

the conversation, allowing the words to pass through her unheard. Instead, she relaxed her mind, leaving it open to impressions beyond words.

This was how she had found the last source of the water. She had been half-dead from thirst, mentally numb, and lost in the desert with Vivian when a quiet impulse led her right to the lifesaving well.

And that impulse came back. A feeling of vague certainty came to her, like walking in the dark in a familiar house, and she said, "To the right, a little farther on."

Grunt angled the Land Rover to the right, and after another kilometer, Jaxon spied a series of low, rocky hills.

"There," she said. "Somewhere in there."

As they approached, she grew even more certain, pointing to one hill in particular. Soon, they spied dark shapes amid the sandblasted stones.

"Walls," Otto said. "Just like in the last place."

They pulled up at the edge of what they could now see was the ruins of a village. Jaxon could tell immediately that it had once been a home of her people, not just because of her gut feeling that this was the place with the well, but by the way the village was constructed. The walls had crumbled and stood only a foot or two high above the sand. Even so, she could see how the houses clustered together, sharing common walls and opening out onto little courtyards where neighbors could spend time with each other.

About half a kilometer to the west stood the ruins of a larger building.

"I bet that was the actual caravanserai," Elaine said, pointing to it. "Our people worked there with the regular humans but lived here with their own kind."

"Smart," Mateo said with a nod.

Everyone got out, looking around quietly. The sun beat down, and the wind whistled through the ruins. Winston put a hand on the top of one of the collapsed walls.

"See this?" he said, tapping the glossy surface of the top stone. "This is called desert varnish, created by the windblown sand rubbing against the surface of the rock. This basalt is some of the hardest rock there is, and it takes thousands of years to make a gloss like this."

"And it's on the exposed, inner part of the wall," Yuhle said, peering at it through the cracks in his glasses. "Which means the wall collapsed thousands of years ago."

"So just how old is this place?" Jaxon asked.

"If we only knew," Elaine said. She sat half in and half out of the Land Rover, still too tired to walk. "It could be from a hundred thousand years ago, maybe more."

Jaxon felt a little shiver at the thought of so much time. What were her little troubles and anxieties compared to all this?

She walked off into the ruins. The others gave her space. As her boots crunched in the sand, she found a little lane between the houses and followed it until it led her to the base of the hill. The last well had been in an undercut at the base of a cliff. Would this be the same?

She came to the remains of a broad square. A larger building stood off to one side. Before her, half filled with sand, she could see an overhang in the side of the hill.

"This must be it!" she called back to the others. "Grab the shovels, and let's dig it out."

They only had three shovels, so Grunt, Mateo, and Winston got to work. Jaxon smiled to herself as she saw that even the scholarly Winston kept up with the hulking mercenary, his Atlantean muscles naturally superior. Mateo, who had obviously had some combat and physical training, beat Grunt by a mile. The Peruvian seemed to get some pleasure from that.

As they dug, Jaxon had a strange feeling that this wasn't quite the right place. That didn't make sense, though, because the side of the hill was the obvious source for a well. She found her eyes straying to the large building to the side of the open square. She wandered over there.

The building was about the size of a small supermarket, with thicker walls and the remains of columns inside. The feeling came stronger here. But why would the water be in this big building? She didn't see a well or the remains of a fountain or anything like that.

She kept searching, the heavy breathing of the men and the sound of the shovels scraping against sand in the background.

At last, those sounds stopped.

"Nothing!" Mateo shouted, tossing his shovel on the ground with disgust. "Not a goddamn thing!"

Grunt and Winston leaned on their shovels, disappointed.

Jaxon went over and saw they had cleared out a little cave set in the hillside. It was smaller than the last one, with no paintings, but like the other well, it had a sunken area that had once held water and a little fissure leading to the subterranean water source. Both were as dry as the desert all around.

"What a waste of time," Grunt said, chugging from a water bottle Otto handed him.

Jaxon sighed. She looked out over the bleak, barren ruins and thought of Trisha, dead before she had ever gotten a chance to really know her. She thought of the Russians too, killed in a fight they probably didn't understand. Yes, it was a waste. A profound waste.

Or was it? That nagging feeling about the big building kept bothering her. On impulse, she picked up the shovel that Mateo had thrown down and walked back to it.

Without her thinking about where she was going, her feet led her to the center of one end of the building, and she began to dig.

CHAPTER 5

AUGUST 19, THE DESERT NORTH OF TIMBUKTU, MALI
2:30 P.M.

"What's she doing?" Otto Heike asked as he watched his girlfriend digging amongst the ruins.

"Working on instinct," Grunt replied, taking another slug of water. "Leave her to it."

The others seemed to agree. They had all sat down in the meager shade provided by the Land Rovers and were eating and drinking. Elaine lay down on the back seat and fell asleep.

Grunt handed him the water bottle, and he took a drink. The water was cool compared to the blistering heat outside, and it sent a sharp jab of pain through his broken tooth.

"Why do you keep rubbing your mouth, pyro?" Grunt asked.

"When I was chewing through Yuhle's ropes, I broke a tooth. One of my incisors."

"You should drink more milk. Gives you strong teeth."

"Ha ha. Very funny. I need to see a dentist."

"Not until we get to a city."

"Don't they have dentists in the villages here?"

Grunt laughed and slapped him on the back, almost making him topple over. "Sure. I've seen one of those country dentists. They heat up a nail until it's red hot then shove it in the gum to kill your nerve. Then they take a pair of pliers and yank out the tooth. Very professional."

"Stop making fun of me. I'm in pain."

"I'm not making fun of you. That's really how they do it here."

"Oh."

Grunt paused, glanced at the others to see they were out of earshot, and asked in a low voice, "So how are you feeling?"

"My tooth hurts. I just told you."

"No, I mean about the firefight."

"I... um..."

"I saw."

"I might not have killed him," Otto said. His voice came out as a squeak.

"You did. Own it. Deal with it."

Otto buried his face in his hand. "Oh God."

"Did you puke? I puked the first time."

Otto nodded. Grunt put a hand on his shoulder.

"No shame, pyro. Every soldier I ever knew freaked out the first few times. Everyone except for Isadore. I should have known how she'd turn out."

"I don't want to be a soldier anymore," Otto whispered.

"Then don't be. You don't have to fight."

"Yeah, I do. All those people chasing us will make me."

Grunt opened his mouth to respond and then closed it without saying anything. They sat watching Jaxon work. Grunt kept his hand on Otto's shoulder. It didn't take the pain and guilt away, but it helped a little.

"Were Dimitri and Nadya among the people who ambushed us?" Otto asked.

"No."

"Maybe we got lucky and they got killed in the fight in Timbuktu," Otto said.

Grunt shook his head. "I didn't see their bodies, so we have to assume they're still alive and kicking. You hardly ever get lucky in this business."

Otto thought of Nadya and how she had led him on. He still felt guilty about it, as if he had cheated on Jaxon, but the guilt of killing a man made that guilt seem like nothing.

If I get out of this alive, I'm never going to set another fire or tell another lie, Otto told himself then wondered if that itself was a lie.

"This world is so messed up," Otto said. "Why does everyone have to make it worse?"

Grunt squeezed his shoulder.

"I feel sorry for you kids. You got a crap inheritance from us—war, terrorism, overpopulation, the environment all turning to poison. It's a bum deal."

"Maybe my generation will come up with the answers."

Grunt snorted. "Your generation eats Tide pods."

The sound of Jaxon's shovel scraping stone made them look.

"I think I found something," she called.

They hurried over, all except for the healer, Elaine, who remained in an exhausted slumber in the Land Rover.

As they came up to Jaxon, she scraped away more sand to reveal a stone platform about the size of a large dinner table. On the wall behind it, they could see vague fragments of some sort of carved picture, but time had eroded away too much of it to tell what it once depicted.

"What is this? An altar of some kind?" Otto asked.

"It might be more than that," Jaxon said, pointing to a seam around one of the stones. "Get me a crowbar."

Otto hurried to fetch one.

Jaxon gripped the thick metal rod and placed the narrow end into the seam. With a grunt and a heave, she lifted the thick stone square up to reveal a small niche beneath. Inside was a gold box.

"Whoa," Otto said.

"This is powerful. I can feel it," Jaxon said.

With infinite care, she picked out the gold box. It measured about a foot long and a little less in width. An elaborate embossed decoration covered its entire surface, showing a world map with all the continents. They looked a bit skewed, though, and Otto's breath caught when he saw a large island in the middle of Atlantic between Africa and the Americas.

"A map of the world from hundreds of thousands

of years ago," Yuhle said, his words almost silenced by awe.

"And Atlantis is right there where the legends said it was," Otto whispered.

Jaxon opened a clasp and lifted the lid. The interior was padded with some plush green material. Inside lay a thin gold chain on which hung a disc of some strange silvery metal. It was about the size of a silver dollar and had a map of the world embossed on it just like the chest. The map was arranged so Atlantis was at the center of the disc.

"What is it?" Otto asked.

"I have no idea," Jaxon replied. She turned to the Atlanteans. "Guys?"

Winston and Mateo shrugged.

"An amazing artifact. It would make a prize find for any museum, but that doesn't help us. We needed more of that water," Yuhle said.

Jaxon set the box down and put the pendant around her neck. She got a confused look on her face, and then her jaw dropped.

"You okay?" Otto asked.

Jaxon turned and faced Mateo and Winston before looking beyond them at the Land Rovers. Then she stared at the horizon in the direction of Timbuktu.

"Jaxon?" Otto said.

Jaxon made a slow turn, gazing out at the horizon in all directions, trembling a little.

She closed her eyes.

"Winston. Mateo. Split up and walk away in different directions. Stop once you get about a hundred yards away."

The two Atlantean men stared at each other for a moment, shrugged, and did as they were asked. Jaxon kept her eyes closed.

Once they stopped, Jaxon pointed right at Winston. "One of you is there."

She turned and pointed directly at Mateo, "And another of you is there."

She spun around several times, eyes still closed, then pointed at them again.

"There and there." She was dead on.

"That must be Elaine over there," she said, pointing right at the Land Rover a few hundred feet away.

She pointed to the south. "Timbuktu is that way." Then to the southwest. "Another settlement of Atlanteans is that way." Then to the due west. "And a big group of Atlanteans, probably that prison camp, is that way. I can even sense that they're much farther away than the Atlanteans in Timbuktu."

"How is that possible?" Otto said, looking at the scientists. They had no answer.

Winston and Mateo walked back to her.

"What a perfect thing for a Keeper of the Texts," Winston said. "You can find any lost members of our people and bring them back into the fold."

Jaxon opened her eyes. They sparked with excitement. "We've been so scattered for so long, but now we can connect everybody!"

"How far can you sense them?" Winston asked.

"I'm not sure exactly. I can tell if one person is closer than the other, and if they're near or far, but not how many miles or anything like that. I also couldn't tell who was who when you two guys split up. That big concentration to the west feels like it's on the borderline of what I can sense, and I kinda get the impression that I'm only feeling that because there are so many of our people there."

"Those refugees said the camp was just north of Tidjikja. I'll get the map," Vivian said, hurrying off. She returned a minute later and spread out the topo map.

"Wow, honey, if your instinct is correct, you can spot a community of Atlanteans from nearly a thousand kilometers away. That's almost six hundred miles."

Otto let out a low whistle.

Jaxon beamed. "This is even better than finding the water!"

"We need some of that water too," Grunt said. "Getting your people out of that camp in Tidjikja won't be a picnic."

More fighting, Otto thought with a shudder.

Mateo looked back at the Land Rovers, concern engraved on his dark features. "Elaine is a pretty good healer, as you saw, but there are limits to how much she can do. I've seen her overextend herself like this before. She's out for the rest of the day. Plus, we could use some of that water if she gets hurt."

"We'll go back to the well I discovered in Mauritania and get as much as we want," Jaxon said. "Then drive straight on and bust them out of that camp."

Grunt put out his hands. "Now wait a minute. We don't know what we're up against. They've probably taken hundreds of people. That means a lot of guards. They'll have machine guns and maybe even some tanks just for chuckles."

Mateo glared at him. "Yeah, but we're going anyway."

Grunt met his gaze. "Yeah, we are, but we've got

to think this through, or we'll all end up dead, and that won't be a help to your people."

Jaxon shook her head, her face stony with worry. "There's also the problem that all the Atlanteans have been rounded up, so we can't stop anywhere. If the locals see us, they'll call the cops."

Mateo shrugged. "We'll avoid the towns, any settled area. And if we do need to stop, the three of us will cover up and stay in the Land Rovers. The real problem comes once we get to that prison camp."

Otto had a sudden thought. "What if General Meade is there?"

"Why would he be?" Jaxon said.

"Yuhle and Yamazaki say that he's making his own Atlanteans now. Brett's blood proved it," Otto said, and his heart twinged at the hurt that came onto Jaxon's face. "What if this roundup is part of his plan?"

"What do you mean?" Winston demanded.

"He wanted to take Jaxon as a sort of lab rat. He didn't get her, so why not get a bunch more Atlanteans in a country where no one will care all that much and the outside world won't even notice? He could use them as test samples or maybe get them under his power somehow."

Grunt went pale. "Oh hell."

Otto bit his lip. Grunt didn't look scared very often, and anytime he did, that meant the situation was seriously bad.

He remembered how Brett had fought. The guy had thrown Jaxon around like a rag doll, and when Grunt and Vivian had opened up on him with their AK-47s, he took dozens of shots in the chest before he went down. The guy had actually walked into the storm of bullets as though he had been walking into a hard wind.

Otto shuddered. *Imagine a whole army of people like that! You could take over the world.*

Vivian brushed a lock of blond hair out of her eyes and said, "General Meade heads a team that oversees American military operations in North Africa. Now it all makes sense."

Everyone fell silent for a moment, thinking of the horrible possibilities.

Vivian went on. "This changes nothing," she said with a hard edge to her voice. "Those people need to be freed, and we're the only ones to do it. I'd be glad if we found General Meade there. That guy's day of reckoning is long overdue."

They sat down together away from the sun, under the shade of a tarpaulin. Even in the shade, the heat pounded on them. After they studied the topo map for a time to estimate how long the trip would take, they went through their supplies. The two scientists checked the food, water, and fuel while the mercenaries and Mateo checked the weapons.

"We have enough food and water for two weeks," Yuhle announced once they all sat down again. "And enough fuel to get there and back."

"I got a bunch of spare fuel from the Land Rover that got hit," Mateo said. "We'll have plenty. And enough weapons for everyone."

Grunt nodded. "I stripped a bunch of AK-47s and ammo from our friends back there. I took that RPG too. It's only got five rounds left, but it packs a punch."

"I'm trained in using one," Mateo said.

Grunt looked at him. "It's a Russian model. They don't train for that in the US Army."

"I wasn't in the US Army," the Atlantean said.

"Were you in any other army?" Vivian asked.

"Only my people's army."

"The Atlanteans trained you how to shoot a rocket-propelled grenade?" Otto said, his eyebrows going up.

Mateo met his gaze. "They trained me in a lot of things."

"What can you do besides that?" Otto asked.

Mateo got a hard gleam in his eye. "What do you mean by that?"

"Every Atlantean has a special power. Jaxon can make plants grow. Winston does that weird hypnotism thing. What can you do?"

"None of your business, kid."

Otto grew angry. "You joking? We're taking on a Third World army, and you're telling me it's none of my business?"

"Calm down, pyro. Spill it, Mateo. We need to know."

Mateo paused for a second then shrugged. "I'm stronger and faster than most Atlanteans."

"He makes regular Atlanteans look like regular people," Winston said.

"Well, that could come in handy, but we don't even know what we're going to face over there," Otto said. "We need a plan."

"How can we make a plan when we've never seen this place?" Jaxon asked.

Grunt sighed and stood up. "By going and taking a look."

CHAPTER 6

AUGUST 21, NOUAKCHOTT AIRPORT, MAURITANIA
9:40 A.M.

General Corbin stepped off the plane in Nouak-chott, the capital of Mauritania. General Meade walked just in front of him since, officially, he was in charge as the commander overseeing North African relations. Orion came right behind them, getting suspicious looks from the Mauritanian soldiers standing at attention on either side of the red carpet that had been laid out for them on the tarmac.

A pair of generals and a guy in a suit, no doubt a politician, stood waiting for them at the end of the carpet. General Corbin snorted. One of the generals was older and getting fat. The other was young with hard features. Both had crisp uniforms bedecked with so many glittering medals they looked as if they were generating their own solar power. Third World generals loved getting medals; it was a status thing. But what were they getting them for? Dealing with a few hostile tribes and the occasional Islamic terrorist? He wondered if they had received medals for rounding up the Atlanteans and decided not to ask.

General Meade stopped in front of the VIPs and snapped off a salute. Corbin held his breath. His artificial Atlantean had been carefully prepared for this, but Corbin still wasn't sure how well he'd do.

"Pleased to meet you again, General Meade," the politician said.

After a pause, Meade said, "And good to see you, too, Vice President Salek."

That's a relief. The memory is still good, Corbin thought.

"We are surprised and delighted by your visit," the vice president went on. "These are generals Haidallah and Teyib."

Corbin had already looked up the key players in this out-of-the-way country. The gray-haired General Haidallah was head of internal security and a survivor of several coups and political purges, while the younger General Teyib was a rising star in the power structure. Both were as corrupt as sin.

Meade gave them a salute that they returned. Then the general turned to Corbin and Orion.

"This is General Arnold Corbin, who is working on a project I think you will find of interest, and this is an agent we call Orion."

Salek did not quite manage to keep a poker face. "One of the People of the Sea."

"That's what we've come to talk to you about," Meade said.

Corbin cut in. This next part would require subtlety and quick wits, both of which Meade now sadly lacked.

"It has come to our attention that you have rounded up the People of the Sea because you saw them as a security risk." Corbin knew that wasn't the real reason, but he still needed to suss out their true motives. He saw Vice President Salek stiffen, so he hastened to add, "I'm glad you're keeping this nation stable, sir. It's vital to the stability of the whole region. But we'd like to speak more of this matter. We have a proposal that might be of interest to you."

The politician grinned. "But of course. And I am sure you'd like to get out of the heat. Much more summery than your California, no?"

"As a military man, I'm accustomed to all sorts of weather," Corbin said.

As a military man, this uniform is suffocating me. It's amazing their soldiers don't go into battle naked, he added silently.

The vice president and the two generals led them to a meeting room at the airport. All three spoke English fairly well. Like many of the elite in this country, they had been educated in Europe. These men had plenty of money, while most of their people lived in poverty.

They all sat down. An air conditioning unit purred in the background. A servant handed out bottled water. They all looked at each other uncertainly. It had been a long time since Mauritania had been visited by two American generals. In the grand scheme of things, it simply wasn't that important. Until now. Corbin decided to make the opening move.

"First, let me say that you should have no concerns about my assistant Orion here. He is a special operative and loyal to me. He doesn't have any loyalty to the People of the Sea or any of their terrorist organizations."

"Ah, my good friend," Vice President Salek said. "I am glad you see the problem with these people.

Our neighbors to the south think they are a harmless minority who keep to themselves, but they have caused us no end of trouble. And now I hear reports from Mali that they are causing trouble there too. Soon they will be as much trouble as the Tuaregs."

"The United States is always happy to help allied nations in need," Corbin said, going way beyond what he was authorized to promise. It didn't matter. If this worked out, he wouldn't have to answer to anyone. "I suspect we could solve your problem with both the People of the Sea and the Tuaregs."

The generals' eyes gleamed. Military aid meant money that could be skimmed off the top. It was amazing what sins you could hide in military budgets. Corbin had become an expert on that, although he suspected these two jokers could teach him a thing or two.

General Haidallah leaned forward, his paunch pressing against the table. General Corbin tried to hide his disgust. Military men should never let themselves get out of shape, although he suspected this character was just as sharp and as dangerous as he had always been.

"As I am sure you are aware," General Haidallah said, "our country is mostly trackless desert. Finding the rebels is not easy, and we lack the funds to launch our own spy satellites."

"We can help with satellite imagery," General Corbin said. In fact, he had no authority to make such a promise, but that would all come in time.

They spent some time discussing technical details until General Teyib cut in impatiently.

"Finding the rebels is important, but once we do, we need to defeat them."

General Corbin took the hint. "I'm sure we can get the Pentagon to approve some increased military funding. Perhaps thirty million dollars for this year? After that, we can work on an increase, depending on results."

Their eyes lit up. Even if they skimmed only a modest ten percent off that budget, they'd each get to build a new palace.

"You will get your results," General Haidallah said.

Corbin did not doubt it. The Tuaregs were a threat to their supremacy. While siphoning off foreign aid was their main goal, getting rid of the rebels came a close second.

A brief technical conversation followed, during which Corbin noticed a slow smile spreading across the vice president's face. Corbin decided to cut to the chase.

"Mr. Vice President, while the United States is happy to provide this help, we, too, are concerned about the People of the Sea. We are glad that you are getting them under control and would like to visit this camp you have built for them in Tidjikja."

"And perhaps take a few away with you?" Vice President Salek's smile had reached its widest point.

Corbin shifted in his seat. "Well, if that would be possible."

"To poke and prod in a laboratory somewhere?"

"Whatever gave you that idea?"

The politician put his hands on the table. "General Corbin, let me tell you a story. As you have no doubt read in your dossier on me, I studied business at the London School of Economics. I got to learn a great deal about how a First World country operates. It was quite a change from the way things work here. Here, I am rich and powerful, but compared with the English upper class, I am a beggar. And trust me when I say that no one is better at teaching you your place than the English upper class. Now, once, on summer vacation, when I was just twenty years old, I traveled to India. Like most young people, I wanted to see the world. Mauritanians are no different, but few ever have a chance to go farther than a hundred kilometers from the village where they were born. I travelled all around India and, of course, visited the famous Taj Mahal."

"You are a lucky man. I've never had a chance to go there," Corbin said, not sure where this was headed.

"Indeed, lucky. It was built by a great Muslim ruler as a monument to his beloved dead wife. One of the most beautiful buildings in the world. Even the Christians admit that. But what affected me most was not the building itself, but what is behind it. Do you know what is behind the Taj Mahal, General Corbin?"

"No."

"Of course you don't. It never makes it into any of the pictures. Behind it is a river, and on the other bank of the river is a peasant's farm field. As I sat on the riverbank, looking up at the beauty of the Taj Mahal, my eyes kept straying to the opposite bank. A woman was filling a bucket in the river and then walking up the riverbank to water the rows of budding plants in her field. She had no pump, no hose, just this bucket, which could water perhaps a couple of meters of one row of plants. The field was a large one, with many rows, and so she kept going back to the river, filling her bucket, and watering another tiny portion of her crop. Back and forth she went. I watched her for an hour, and she got barely a tenth of that field watered. She must have been at it all day. And then the next day, she would have to do it again."

"Quite a contrast to the beauty of the building," General Corbin said.

Vice President Salek tapped his fingers on the table. "Indeed. That day taught me more about how the world works than all those years of study in London. A great symbol of beauty, wealth, and power, and next to it a miserable life of drudgery and toil. One wonders what that woman thinks of the Taj Mahal. Does she admire its beauty? Does she notice it at all? Perhaps she is too tired. Perhaps the world has killed her thoughts already."

"Mr. Vice President, about the camp at—"

The politician raised a hand, and Corbin fell silent. There was something powerful about this man. Corbin realized he had underestimated him.

"Ten years later, on my honeymoon, I went back to the Taj Mahal, General Corbin. It is a popular place for Indians to go on their honeymoon since it is so romantic, and so I decided to take my wife there. Of course, I went to the back and looked across the river. The field was still there, and a woman was still watering the furrows, but I do not think it was the same woman. She looked younger than I remembered. I think that it must be her daughter, and the first woman I saw had died, worn out by the cruelty of the world. Perhaps working ten-hour days in the hot sun next to the world's most beautiful building sapped her will to live. What do you think of that, my powerful American general?"

General Corbin paused, trying to think of a politic response. "I think that's a bit of a tragedy."

Vice President Salk slapped his hand on the table, the sound loud in the otherwise silent room. "A tragedy? Perhaps. But it is the way of the world. The peasants toil and suffer so that a select few can build great monuments and be remembered. It is how countries work. Even in your great democracies, you have people working long hours in supermarkets and restaurants while a few live the lives of billionaires or go to the space station. It is the same between countries too. Some achieve great things, while others toil and suffer and die young. It is like America and Mauritania, General Corbin."

"Now, Mr. Vice President, the United States respects—"

"The United States respects nothing!" Salek screamed.

Deadly silence fell around the conference table. Salek took a sip of water, collected himself, and went on.

"You Americans see yourself as the Taj Mahal and countries like mine as that peasant woman. Well, we have grown something in our field, haven't we? Something you want. Something the Russians want too."

General Corbin tensed. "The Russians?"

General Haidallah, head of internal security, chuckled. "Do you think you are the only nation that gathers intelligence in this region? Do not forget that we live here, and we have methods of learning things far better than your satellite photos. The Russians have been interested in the People of the Sea for a long time, and now the Americans are too, but while the Russians are studying them with the help of their embassy, the Americans go about it more secretly. I suspect that only one faction in your government is studying the People of the Sea and hiding its actions from all the other factions. I also suspect that both you and the Russians are interested in the People of the Sea's magical powers."

"There is no such thing as magic," General Corbin said.

"You say that because you do not live here, my good general. They do indeed have magical powers and are stronger and faster than regular people. This must be because they are descended from the people of Atlantis. Do not look surprised. We know that too. What we don't know is what you and the Russians plan to do with them. Use them as weapons against each other or to fight against the alien invasion that is sure to come?"

General Corbin blinked. So this guy had picked up enough of the fake intelligence reports on UFOs to believe the lies he had been spreading all these years? Perhaps he could use that to his advantage.

"Indeed, Mr. Vice President, the United States is very concerned about the alien threat. We have no technology to fight such a power, and we need the Atlanteans as soldiers to help us save the world."

"So you say." Salek did not sound convinced. "The Russians say many fine and noble things too. But you have to understand that the peasant woman does not trust the man in the Taj Mahal and will never trust him. How could she when their lives are so different? You come here to our desert country that is cursed with no natural resources and claim you want to help us. Really, you only want to help yourselves. Well, we have something you want, and that will go to the highest bidder."

Vice President Salek pressed a buzzer in front of him, and a door to the right of him opened. In stepped several local soldiers. Then Corbin saw who came with them, and he nearly fell out of his chair with shock.

It was Nadya Antipova and Dimitri Rublev, the Russian agents who had caused so much trouble in Mali.

Nadya slunk up to the vice president. "So good of you to allow us to have this little chat."

She put a hand on his cheek. Salek flushed, but his eyes remained calculating. Nadya turned to General Corbin.

"Now then, General, let the bargaining begin."

CHAPTER 7

AUGUST 26, THE DESERT DUE EAST OF
TIDJIKJA, MAURITANIA
10:00 P.M.

So far, things had gone well. Jaxon had led them
unerringly to the well of original water, where they
had filled up several large jugs. Instead of the few
precious canteens they had taken away before, now
they carried several dozen gallons of the miraculous
healing liquid.

Winston, Elaine, and Mateo had marveled at the
cave paintings showing Atlantean history.

Taking up the cave wall behind the well of
healing water, the paintings were even more beautiful and moving than Jaxon remembered.

The entire wall was covered in a long-lasting paint the scientists had told her was made from grinding up minerals to create a paint that had the consistency of nail polish. Sheltered from the elements in this cave, its colors had remained bright and its images clear despite the millennia that had passed.

Dark-skinned figures with dreadlocks and bright-blue dots for eyes wore robes of brilliant yellow, shimmering blue and gold, or deep indigo as the Tuaregs favored.

Winston, being the scholarly one among her three new friends, had gone over the scenes in detail.

"Here's the main city of Atlantis," he said, pointing to a cluster of magnificent buildings with pillars of white marble. The walls were also of marble, and both were decorated with flakes of gold. "It was the capital of the world for a time, the center of all the greatest science and art. See how they've put flakes of gold into the paint? It's said that our ancestors had a method of actually mixing gold into stone to get this effect. Those pillars really would have had gold flakes in them, and not just set into them, but actually integral with the stone itself."

"How could they do that?" Elaine said in her Southern drawl.

Winston grimaced. "No one knows. It's yet another thing we have lost." Then his face brightened. "Ah! Look at this."

He pointed to a bird's-eye view of the city, consisting of three rings of buildings divided by canals. A semicircular port took up one side, where tiny boats sailed on a blue sea. Jaxon hadn't noticed during her first visit, but the buildings were highly detailed. They weren't just a series of squares and rectangles as someone would draw to make a schematic of a city, but each had its own individual shape. The boats, too, were each drawn individually.

"It's like a snapshot from my drone," Elaine said.

"I wonder if they didn't do something similar for this image," Winston said. "I can't recall anything in the ancient texts about flying machines or photography, but considering all the other things our ancestors could do, I wouldn't put it past them."

To the right of the city was another scene in close-up showing figures standing in circles around men and women with their hands raised in the air as if they were delivering speeches.

"The time of the Great Division," Winston said. "When we had grown corrupt and greedy. Some angry young leaders wanted to use our might to conquer the world and enslave the regular humans, while most of our people simply wanted to live a life of lazy pleasure and dissipation. The traditionalists stuck to the founding principles of our civilization, which was to live in peace and slowly spread our knowledge to the rest of the world as each lesser civilization became ready for it."

"And they all ended up fighting," Mateo said, pointing to the next scene—a huge battle painted with a blood-red background. Dismembered and decapitated bodies lay everywhere.

The last scene showed the one part of this story that even most regular humans knew—God's wrath at the arrogance and corruption of Atlantis. Giant waves broke the city apart and swept thousands of tiny figures out to sea. Off to one side, a few ships made their escape.

"So the faction that wanted to spread out across the world got their wish," Winston said, pointing to them. "But not in the way they wanted. And they didn't get to spread all that much of their knowledge because most of it sank beneath the waves. Nobody won that civil war. Just goes to show that violence is never the answer."

Winston gave Mateo a significant look. Mateo snorted.

"Sometimes violence is the only answer. How

else are we going to get our people free—walk up to that concentration camp, holding a bouquet of roses?"

Winston studied him for a moment. "You ever hear the old saying that those who don't learn from history are doomed to repeat it?"

Mateo sneered. "That's a human saying, not an Atlantean one."

"We are human," Jaxon said.

"You'll learn one day, kid," Mateo said, walking out of the cave and shaking his head.

After that, they had stuck to the desert, avoiding any settlements that showed up on their maps and any open stretch between settlements where they might bump into other vehicles. Their days were lonely ones of endless driving through sun-scorched nothingness—no towns, no outposts, not even any tire tracks in the sand.

In this bleak wilderness, there was nothing to do but talk. Jaxon hadn't seen television in weeks, had lost her iPad in a sandstorm, and didn't even have any music. Instead, she had a circle of loyal friends and some new Atlantean acquaintances who knew far more than she did about her heritage. She was the most cut off and the most connected she had ever been in her entire life.

One day while riding with Winston, she asked him about their first meeting back in Timbuktu.

"You mentioned you wanted to take me down to Gambia. Why?"

"The Gambia is a vital place in our past—indeed, the past for all of West Africa. It doesn't look like much, just a little strip of a country on either side of the River Gambia far to the south of here where there's actually water and plants instead of all this depressing desert, but it's played a major role in history."

"Did some of us land there after Atlantis sank?"

"Indeed, we did, because the River Gambia reaches far into West Africa. Being seafarers, we settled at the mouth of that river so we could trade with the interior and still be by the ocean. I suppose we probably had a trading station there even before Atlantis was consumed by the waves. We had trading stations all over, although their exact locations are lost. Like with so many other places where our refugees landed, we played a great role in founding the later civilizations. You can see elements of Atlantean influence in some of the greatest of West African art styles, such as the Benin bronzes and the masks of Cameroon."

"I didn't do well in art history."

"That's not the sort of thing you would have been taught anyway. Did you get much education on the slave trade?"

"A bit." Those lessons, at least, she had paid attention to.

"Then you know that the River Gambia was a main trading center in human flesh. Arab and African slave traders raided the weaker tribes in the interior and sold the captives to rulers on the west coast or, later, to European companies who then shipped them to the New World."

"Did any of us get shipped as slaves?"

Winston made a face. "Perhaps, but there's a more shameful element to this story. One of the biggest slave traders in the seventeenth century was one of us."

"What?"

Jaxon glanced at Mateo, since he disagreed with pretty much everything Winston said. But he wasn't disagreeing this time. Instead, he looked embarrassed. Winston went on.

"We don't know his real name, only the French name he went by—Mars Sans Pitié. That means 'Mars the Ruthless.'"

"Mars, as in the god of war? Like Ares? Great, so

I share a name with a slave trader. Thanks for the history lesson."

"Sorry. History is full of uncomfortable facts. I bet they didn't tell you in school that Africans participated in the slave trade. Or that American corporations sold technology to Hitler before America entered World War II. The textbooks like everything neat and tidy, but if you read real history, things get very ugly very quickly. Even good things are ignored, like the fact that many Viking warriors were women and that they had the first democracy in medieval Europe."

"So tell me more about this Atlantean slave trader. What's he got to do with all this?" Jaxon asked as a massive weight of disappointment threatened to crush her. She had hoped that her people might be different, that their mistakes and evils were all in the ancient past.

"Mars Sans Pitié could control people. His talent was much like mine, although he used it for foul purposes. This helped him set up his slave empire. He made a fortune selling fellow humans and had a whole army of guards under his control."

"Wait, how could he control a whole army? You can't do that, can you?"

Winston shook his head. "I could barely control

those two policemen back in Araouane. I doubt his power was much stronger than mine, but he had help. He had an ancient device, one of the greatest accomplishments of our people, that could magnify our individual talents. We don't know what it looks like or even what it was called. All that knowledge has been lost. But we suspect it's still hidden somewhere in his old fort at the mouth of the River Gambia."

"If it's been hidden for all these years, how are we going to find it?"

Elaine nudged her. "Didn't you find that amulet in the ruins? You're the one we need. We always knew that."

"And when you magnify your powers, you will be able to find all the other lost technology hidden around the world," Mateo said, his crystal-blue eyes lighting up. "We can finally rebuild."

Jaxon shuddered and looked out the window. Why was all this responsibility being put on her?

After several days of searching in the barren waste, Grunt made contact with the Tuareg rebels and told them what had happened to the Atlanteans. Their leader, Agerzam, already knew about the roundup, but he had not known the reasons behind it.

Agerzam was outraged. He pledged to help in any way he could. "The government's enemies are my enemies," he swore, his high-class English accent, developed while studying at Oxford University, at odds with his desert robes and the AK-47 slung across his back. "The People of the Sea have never oppressed my people, and if they are now oppressed by those who oppress us, they are our brothers and sisters."

Noble words, Jaxon mused, but they masked a more practical side. If the Tuaregs could get the People of the Sea on their side with their fabled magical powers, they would have earned a valuable ally. Plus, exposing these crimes to the world would certainly undermine the government's position and perhaps force the major powers to the negotiating table.

They hid at night with a band of Tuareg fighters in a rough area of stony hills and gritty sand dunes in a stretch of the most barren desert Jaxon had ever seen, and she had seen way too much desert in the past few months. Her companions and Agerzam hunched over a satellite photo of the prison camp that the Tuareg leader had laid out on the sand. They used only a single flashlight to see by. Even this far from civilization, you could not assume you were safe from prying eyes.

The satellite photo showed the prison camp laid out on the pale brown of the desert sands. It was square in shape, with guard towers on each corner and what looked like a barbed-wire fence enclosing the whole place. A couple of long buildings to one side, also enclosed in barbed wire, were probably barracks for the soldiers. The rest of the space was taken up by a giant tent village. They hadn't even given the Atlanteans proper shelter.

"Nice image," Grunt said. "Taken by one of the newer-model satellites. Where did you get this?"

"We have connections, my friend," Agerzam said.

Grunt ran a finger along one edge, where a portion of the photo had been cut off. "And you don't want me to know what those connections are, eh? I bet this missing part had the technical data. What language was it in—English, French, or Russian?"

Agerzam shrugged. "What does it matter, my friend?"

"You know you can crop a photo before printing it out," Otto said.

"I'm too busy fighting for my people's freedom to learn Photoshop."

Agerzam and Otto chuckled. Otto seemed more relaxed now. He had been slowly recovering from the shock of his first kill, and it was good to see him smiling again. Jaxon felt bad to have brought him into all this, but it had been necessary.

Why is it any time I do something necessary, innocent people get hurt? she asked herself.

She stowed that question in the back of her mind and focused on the map. They had work to do.

"As you can see, we have a tough situation," Agerzam said. "I managed to get a scout nearby one night. He didn't dare get too close, but he confirmed there are machine guns in each of those towers. Here is the gate"—Agerzam pointed to a pair of closely set towers along one side of the enclosure—"and there are machine guns and rocket-propelled grenades in both of those towers."

"So we're totally outgunned," Jaxon said. That was par for the course. They'd been outgunned since the start of this thing. Agerzam laid out another satellite image, this one on a larger scale.

"The prison camp is twenty kilometers from town in the middle of a flat valley. A few hills to the east offer some cover, but this square shape here is a watchtower set atop the tallest hill so they can watch for any approach from that direction and radio for help if they need it."

Jaxon picked up the image of the camp and pointed to a small square building between the two large barracks.

"What's this?" her voice came out strained but in control. When she had first seen the image of the prison camp, she had burst into tears.

Agerzam shook his head. "We don't know. Our scout couldn't get close enough to see it."

"Those are civilian cars, right?" Jaxon said, pointing to the little white vehicles parked next to the building, so unlike the camouflaged military vehicles.

"You have a good eye, young lady," Agerzam said, nodding with approval. "Yes, perhaps that's some sort of research laboratory."

"Lab rats," Jaxon spat.

Agerzam looked at her. "Not for long."

"So how do we get in?" Otto said. "Even if you bring enough Tuaregs to bust into that place, a bunch of Atlanteans are going to get killed in the crossfire."

Jaxon bit her lip. Otto had put into words what had been worrying her ever since she had first laid eyes on this image.

Agerzam grinned. "Desert warfare requires subtlety and guile. We have always been outnumbered by the governments that have tried to crush us, but we have always held our own by being smarter and more resourceful than they are. In an hour or so, the solution will come."

The solution came in the form of a Mauritanian Army Jeep and truck that arrived in camp with their lights off. The men inside all wore military uniforms but had distinctive Tuareg features.

"Nice one, Agerzam," Grunt said, slapping his old friend on the back. "Should I even ask how you got these?"

"No, you should not, my brother."

"Got some spare uniforms for us?"

"Yes."

They examined the vehicles. Agerzam's men had done well. There wasn't a single bullet hole on either the Jeep or the truck. However they had gotten them, they hadn't spilled blood for them. Good. Jaxon didn't want anyone killed unless it was absolutely necessary. Grunt told her the vehicles were both older models but in decent shape. The radios worked, too, so they could listen in on army communications, although no doubt Agerzam already had that capability.

"So what's the plan?" Grunt asked. "Sneak in and take them by surprise? Even if we fill up the back of this truck with men, we'll be outnumbered."

"There's an officer always by the gate. If we capture him and his men, then perhaps we can negotiate," Agerzam said.

"Perhaps," Grunt said, sounding doubtful. "But even if we get them to hand over the People of the Sea, how are we going to get them out of here? There are hundreds of them!"

"More trucks are on the way, my brother, enough to take them all."

"We'll be sitting ducks if they decide to send the air force after us. Mauritania doesn't have much of an air force by Western standards, but it's good enough to take out a column of trucks in the open desert."

Agerzam's face clouded. "I do not have a solution for that other than to do this at night and then split up and hope for the best."

Jaxon frowned at him. "Well, that's great, but even if by some miracle we all get away, what then? The government will just try to round everyone up again. With the mess we made back in Mali, my people won't be able to get out that way. The army will never let them across the border. And Morocco is too far. So what do we do?"

Everyone fell silent for a moment, thinking. Otto spoke first.

"Why don't we get some international media attention? Tell the world what's happening here!"

"Yeah," Jaxon put in. She had been thinking the same thing.

"Because nobody gives a damn," Agerzam said. "My people have been oppressed for decades. Have you ever read about it in the newspapers? When I lived in Oxford, I used to read all the Western papers. The *Guardian*, the *Telegraph*, the *International Herald Tribune, Le Monde Diplomatique*. They hardly ever mentioned Africa, and when they did, they only showed their ignorance or their greed. Big-game hunting and oil concessions were all they ever talked about. If the Tuaregs had oil or uranium, people would care, but we don't. The People of the Sea have even less."

Jaxon turned to the three other Atlanteans. "We could tell them everything. Make the world understand just how special we are and just how much humanity needs us. They should know everything."

The three Atlanteans got a guarded look on their faces.

"What do you mean, 'everything'?" Mateo asked.

"Everything. About us. About where we're from. About what we can do."

Winston looked horrified. "Oh Jaxon, I don't think that's a good idea."

Agerzam looked from Jaxon to Winston and back again. "What are you talking about? How are the People of the Sea so special?"

Jaxon took a deep breath. "We're—"

"This conversation stops now!" Mateo snapped.

Jaxon threw up her hands in disgust and walked off.

━━━

Jaxon stood out of the light, staring up at the brilliant night sky. The stars were so bright here, sharp pinpoints of light that almost hurt to look at. Perhaps there was peace out there between the stars, where there was no one to bother you and nobody who wanted to use you for their own ends.

A faint star moved between the others. Silently, it arced across the sky from east to west. A satellite. Vivian had pointed them out to her before. It could even be a spy satellite checking out this position.

Great. Even the night sky is against us.

"You can't trust their kind," a voice said behind her. Mateo.

"Where do you get off talking like that?" Jaxon snapped. "After all the crap they've thrown at us, you want to turn around and act the same way?"

The Peruvian snorted. "I'm just being realistic. Any time one of them has helped one of us, it's been for their own damned reasons."

"My friends are different."

Mateo gave her a look as if she were a silly little kid. "Of course they are."

"They've put their lives on the line for me. Do you think any of them want to be here? They're helping me because they believe in what we're doing. And they care about me."

Jaxon thought of Otto. Their relationship had been cooling for some time now. He spent more time with that crazy mercenary, Grunt, than he did with her. Perhaps he needed a father figure more than he needed a girlfriend. He'd had plenty of girls. He'd never had a father in his life.

Mateo shook his head, the movement almost invisible in the darkness. "Even the well-intentioned ones end up disappointing us."

CHAPTER 8

AUGUST 27, THE PRISON CAMP A FEW
MILES EAST OF TIDJIKJA, MAURITANIA
5:45 P.M.

General Corbin looked around the prison camp with
distaste. He had seen many godforsaken places in his
time, but this was the worst. The giant barbed-wire
enclosure stood on a barren, windswept plain with
no shade and no source water. A few large water
trucks were parked just inside the gate, but Corbin
calculated that they barely provided enough to drink,
let alone wash. The food situation didn't look much
better.

The government's plan was obvious—keep the
Atlanteans barely alive so they couldn't cause any

trouble. It seemed to be working. The people he saw sitting around the tents looked ragged and despondent. He suspected that they'd still be capable of launching a prison break if they could muster the courage. With their speed and strength, they could overwhelm the guards and tear up the fence in minutes.

They'd lose a lot of people from those machine-gun towers, though, and with all the children and old people here, the healthier Atlanteans wouldn't want to risk it. Besides, there was nowhere for them to run.

So the Atlanteans were under control. Good. He estimated they numbered about six hundred. A few hundred more had fled to neighboring countries, and no doubt some were hiding out, but the government had captured enough of them to make a decent genetic sample of their population.

The only problem was, he wasn't sure he'd get that chance, not with those Russian agents here. Vice President Salek was showing both groups around as if he were some sort of used-car salesman. Corbin had no doubt he'd sell to the highest bidder, and the Russians had Moscow behind them. Corbin only had his secret funds and no way to get more on such short notice.

Salek, flanked by the two generals and several

heavily armed soldiers, led them into a small building with several civilian vehicles parked next to it. Inside, they saw what Corbin had suspected and what he had feared—a small but well-stocked laboratory filled with scientific equipment. Several Mauritanian researchers in lab coats were hard at work. Corbin didn't know much about science, but he had been involved in the Poseidon Project long enough to recognize a genetics lab when he saw one.

"You're creating a genetic database of the Atlantean prisoners," Dimitri Rublev said.

"It is a quick process, or so my scientists tell me," Salek said. "We just need an oral swab from each individual and then put it through the imaging process. When we are done, we will have what the two great powers do not have, the key to unlocking the secret of the race of ancient Atlantis. These are the genes that helped create world civilization, the genes that, if the legends are to be believed, built the greatest civilization of them all. And these genes hold the key to the Atlanteans' magical powers. We have been preparing for this for many years, sending bright university students to train in Europe as genetics experts. Quite an expensive project that I hope will soon pay off."

Dimitri turned to him. "My government will pay handsomely for this information."

"As will mine," General Corbin said.

The vice president nodded, evidently pleased. "I must admit that our president and his cabinet were reluctant to put all our cards on the table, as you say in America. They were worried you might invade in order to take what you want. A single well-supported brigade of either of your armies could do it with ease."

General Corbin cut in. "Mr. Vice President, the United States would never—"

Salek cut him off. "Don't be ridiculous, general. When has your nation not been at war? And as for the Russians"—he gave Dimitri and Nadya a sly look —"they are an equally grave danger to a nation like mine. Nevertheless, I convinced my superiors that we were safe from invasion using a simple economic argument. A cost-benefit analysis, as we economists say. Since you both know what we have to offer, any attempt to take over our country could spark a war between you that neither of you wants or can afford. You've always been content to fight it out with puppet regimes in proxy wars. Oh, very civilized, I must say. Korea. The Arab-Israeli War. The Congo. El Salvador. All wars between Russia and the

United States in which neither of your countries got your hands dirty but in which hundreds of thousands died. And you come here looking at us as barbarians. But now you don't get to do that. One of you will walk away with the contract for the Atlantean genetic code, and there's nothing the other can do about it. So make your bids, ladies and gentlemen, and then get out of my country."

General Corbin cocked his head. "Mr. Vice President, if you weren't enslaving your own people, I'd actually admire you for a patriot."

Salek gave him a level stare. "I have been to New York City as well as the Taj Mahal, General. I have seen how you treat people who have dark skin in your country. Don't talk to me about slavery. These people will be let go once we get what we want. That's better than what you'd do to them."

General Corbin shrugged. He couldn't argue with that.

After a tour of the laboratory that satisfied both General Corbin and the Russians that they'd receive exactly what had been promised, Salek ushered them into the barracks.

"Here we have set aside private quarters for both delegations. I presume you both have encrypted satellite telephones?" Corbin and Nadya nodded.

"Excellent. Then you can call your superiors and discuss the details of what you will offer. It is already getting a bit late, and there have been reports of Tuareg rebels spotted in the area. I suggest we stay here for the night. You will be quite safe, and I assure you the rooms are not bugged. No doubt you have the equipment to check that I am telling the truth. Have a good evening, and I will see you at dinner, where we will resume our little chat. If you need anything, do not hesitate to ask."

Salek and the two generals left. A couple of the guards stayed at the end of the hallway, blocking the only way out. Nadya and Dimitri gave Corbin a suspicious look and went into their room, closing and locking the door behind them.

Corbin turned to Orion. "Stand guard."

Orion didn't respond or even nod. He merely took a position in front of their door and stood at attention. The Mauritanian soldiers at the end of the hallway looked at him uncomfortably. Corbin and General Meade entered the room.

It was a sparse concrete rectangle with four cots and a bureau that reminded him of some of the barracks he'd slept in when he was still a common soldier. It seemed that all armies kept their men in equally ugly quarters. Corbin put his briefcase down on one of the beds and pulled out an electronic detector. After a careful scan of the room, he found Salek had been good to his word. The room wasn't bugged, and there were no hidden cameras. He also checked for holes in the wall, ceiling, and floor. In this electronic age, people often overlooked the simpler, more old-fashioned methods of eavesdropping. He found none of those either. It appeared they had privacy.

General Meade still stood just inside the door, staring at Corbin.

"Lie down on the bed and take a nap or something. You're giving me the creeps," Corbin snapped.

Meade quietly did as he was told.

Shaking his head, Corbin pulled out his satellite phone. It was the latest technology. Not even the Russians or Chinese knew how to hack it, or at least that was the word around the Pentagon. Certainly, Salek and his flunkies weren't up to the challenge.

He put in a call to Dr. Jones. Once he got him on the line and found out that the new subjects were progressing well and that another batch of five teenage runaways had been collected and were getting the same treatment, Corbin outlined what he had learned.

"That's incredible!" Dr. Jones cried. "A once-in-a-lifetime chance. We have to get those data."

"It's going to the highest bidder, and the Russians are going to outbid us."

"Call the Joint Chiefs of Staff and ask for more funding. I'm sure if you explain how important this is, they'll provide more money. I'd be happy to speak with them for you."

"That won't be necessary," Corbin said. Dr. Jones didn't know he had gone rogue. The scientist thought he was working on a top-secret project that had the blessing of the Pentagon. He had been sworn to secrecy, so there was no chance of him giving the game away, but Jones didn't realize just how tight their funding was and how it was impossible to get more at the moment.

"We really need those genetic samples," the scientist continued. "Imagine, a nearly complete genetic sample of the Atlantean population from an entire country! That would bring our research ahead by years."

"How can we get it without paying for it?"

There was a pause at the other end of the line. "What do you mean?"

"We don't have the funds. The Russians will outbid us."

"But I thought—"

"Never mind what you thought. How else can we get it?"

"I don't know. I'm not a computer hacker."

Corbin hung up. His next call was to Operation Bicker. Most of them were simply experienced Internet trolls with dozens of online personalities they used to sway public opinion, but among them were a few skilled hackers. Corbin gave them the location of the camp and asked them to search for the genetics database at the lab computer. They told them they'd get back to him in half an hour.

After half an hour of pacing, he got some bad news.

"I'm sorry, sir," the head of his hacking team said. "We checked for any satellite communications from that camp, and aside from the usual military chatter, there was no computer link. They've done the most basic and foolproof security measure of all—not linking their database to the Internet."

"Then how do they get their information to the central government?" General Corbin asked.

"I guess they save it to an external hard drive and move it manually to the capital. They probably send updates every week or so."

"Can you hack the capital's computers?"

"Which one? The university? The military? The government? Even in a small country like that, the capital has thousands of computers. And if they are being so cautious on your end, I don't think they'd keep the data on an exposed computer in the capital."

General Corbin cursed. After taking a moment to get control of his emotions, he called Dr. Jones again. He explained what the hacker had told him and then said, "The Mauritanians only started this research project a few weeks ago at most. From what I know, genetics testing takes some time. Do you think they already have much information stored in the capital?"

Dr. Jones sounded relieved. "Oh, if it's that recent of a project, they might not have sent an update at all. Usually, with research of this scale, there's a considerable setup time. That politician you told me about is bluffing. He's gathering the data, but he doesn't have it all yet."

General Corbin thought for a moment. "Do we really need this database?" he asked. "We already have the serum to make our own Atlanteans."

"If we have that database, we can refine the serum. Plus, who knows what else we'll discover? We don't know how the Atlanteans create their special powers, for example, and the test subjects don't seem to develop that, at least not in the beginning stages. We haven't had time for a long-term study, of course, so if we—"

"We're not going to have time for a long-term study, so put that out of your mind," General Corbin said. Sooner or later, someone at the Pentagon was going to start asking questions about what he was doing. He needed to strike soon.

Neither spoke for a moment.

At last, Dr. Jones said, "If we don't get the database, it won't be a disaster. We have the serum. I don't know why you're in such a rush, but if we just get a few years, we can make our own database. You can't rush science. Even with the information the Mauritanians have gathered, it would take a year or so just to analyze. So whatever you have planned for the short term, you're only going to get to work with the serum. The artificial Atlanteans will have to do for now."

"What if the Russians get the database?"

"Don't let them." Dr. Jones's voice came out unusually hard. Corbin realized that the scientist's pride was at stake.

These eggheads could be just as competitive as

any athlete or soldier, he thought with a smile. "Yes, but what if they do?"

"You say the sample size is around six hundred?"

"You mean the number of Atlanteans they have here?"

"Yes. There's no way we're going to be able to gather that kind of sample anytime soon. It would take years, and you say you don't have years. It would help if I knew what you wanted to do with all this."

"Never mind that. So are you saying that if the Russians get it, they'd be too far ahead for us to ever catch up?"

"Exactly. They're not as advanced in genetics technology as we are, but with a head start like that, they'd don't need to be."

"So what do you suggest I do?" General Corbin asked, completely at a loss.

"You can't steal it?"

Corbin snorted. This guy was incredible. "I'm at an army base, so no."

"Then send Orion in to destroy it."

The scientist's words came out with that same hardness as before.

General Corbin paused then asked, "You'd destroy a precious, one-of-a-kind scientific database just to keep it from the Russians?"

"Yes."

The general smiled. "Doctor, I underestimated you. Yours is the only solution. I see that now. Have a good day."

General Corbin hung up and got to planning.

CHAPTER 9

AUGUST 27, THE SAHARA DESERT A FEW MILES EAST OF TIDJIKJA, MAURITANIA
11:00 P.M.

It was almost time to launch the attack on the prison camp, and Jaxon had the jitters. She paced back and forth in the darkness. The whole plan sounded stupid, and the getaway even stupider, but she didn't have any better ideas.

The worst of it all was that people were going to get killed. There was no way around that.

Agerzam had already radioed ahead to the prison camp, pretending to be an army officer and saying that the Jeep and truck were coming in. He had explained the unscheduled arrival by blaming the quartermaster at another army base for mixing up deliveries of supplies. He said that since it was so late and he was afraid of the Tuaregs, they wanted to stay at the prison camp overnight for safety. The commander of the camp agreed, not suspecting that the man on the military radio channel was actually the government's public enemy number one.

So in a few minutes, some of Agerzam's men would set out in the Jeep and truck dressed as military. The Atlantis Allegiance and the Atlantis Guard would ride in the back of the truck. They already wore military uniforms. Jaxon's was too long and baggy, and her telltale features remained all too visible. It wasn't much of a disguise, but she and the other Atlanteans and foreigners would hide in the back of the truck so the prison guards wouldn't see their faces.

Elaine had sent up her drone earlier that evening, and it had spotted more vehicles than Agerzam's satellite photo had. They looked both military and civilian. Something was going on in the camp, something unusual. Perhaps Grunt was right and General Meade really had come to visit. She'd like to meet him face to face. He'd been the cause of all her troubles for the last several months, and she had never even laid eyes on him.

Yuhle and Yamazaki were staying behind. Agerzam had wanted to go, but his men refused to allow him, saying he was too important to risk in such a dangerous mission. This led to a long argument in their own language. Jaxon didn't know any of the words but could follow the gist of it easily enough. The Tuareg leader's pride dictated that he should lead his men into battle. He kept gesturing at Vivian, Jaxon, and Elaine as he shouted at his men. Jaxon figured he was saying something like, "You let women fight but not me?"

In the end, his men held their ground and won. This rebel group was no dictatorship, and if the men united around something, the leader had to follow their lead. Agerzam left the circle grumbling and shaking his head.

Another person who would stay behind was Otto. He volunteered to go, but Grunt convinced him to stay behind too. Jaxon got the sense that her boyfriend actually felt relieved not to have to go.

The plan was simple. They'd drive up to the gate, show the identification they'd stolen from the army, and get let in, and from there, they'd play it by ear. With luck, Winston could get the commander under his control and get him to order his men to let the Atlanteans go. Then the column of trucks Agerzam had waiting in the desert nearby would come in and take them away. If they weren't lucky, they might have to shoot it out. Surprise would be on their side, and some of the prisoners would no doubt help, so they stood a good chance of winning.

It would be a bloodbath, though.

A low whistle from the direction of the trucks told her the time had come. She could see no lights over there. The entire camp kept itself in darkness in case the army had scouts out watching.

She paused, took a deep breath, and stared at the sky for a moment.

"Come on, be a hero," she told herself. "It's not like you have any choice."

She walked toward the trucks. Somehow, Otto found her in the dark and cut her off.

"I can come if you want," he said.

"No. You don't need to come, so there's no point you risking your life."

"I don't like sending you into danger all alone."

"I'm hardly alone, Otto, but I know what you mean. Look, Grunt said that it would be better if your place was taken by a trained fighter. We need Winston for his power and Elaine for her healing. Everyone else is a trained fighter."

"You're not."

"No, but it's my fight."

There was a pause. Jaxon tried to read his expression in the darkness but couldn't.

"Yeah, I guess Grunt is right from a tactical viewpoint," Otto said as if he was trying to reassure himself.

Jaxon drew him close and kissed him. She hoped it wouldn't be for the last time.

"Take care," she said.

"You too." Otto walked away and was swallowed by the shadows.

She continued to the trucks, heart beating fast. Everyone had assembled and was busy checking their weapons by the starlight. She found Winston and pulled him aside.

"I just had an idea," she said. "Why don't we get that thing in Gambia first, that artifact the slaver used, and then you could use your power to control all these people's minds. We could just walk them out of that camp!"

Anything to get out of this, she thought.

Winston shook his head slowly, and when he replied, his voice sounded grave. "No, Jaxon. It would take too long to find. Just the trip there and back would take several days, and who knows if we would make it considering all the people hunting us. Whatever our enemies have planned for these captive Atlanteans, they will have done it long before we get back."

Her heart sank. There didn't look like there was any way to avoid this attack. Jaxon studied him. "That's true, but that's not the real reason you don't want to try it, isn't it?"

Winston looked at his feet. "It's a good-enough reason, but you're correct. The truth is I'm afraid. I was always the small child in school, picked on for not being good at games and for not having any parents. Perhaps I developed my particular power just to get the other children to leave me alone. There's a lot of anger in me, just as much as there is in Mateo. I hide it, control it like he should learn to do, but it's still there. If I try to use that artifact, I might become as bad as some of our oppressors."

Jaxon fell silent. Everyone seemed to assume that she'd use this artifact, if they ever found it. But what would that kind of power do to her? Winston talked about being angry, but she'd spent her entire life angry. Most of her childhood, she kept her head down, wanting to be ignored, while all the time quietly seething. Then she had let it all out when she and Brett went hunting criminals together. It sickened her to think about it now. How she had thrilled at the feel of smacking around weaker, regular humans. It didn't matter that they were thugs who deserved to be in jail—hunting them had made her too much like them.

And now she was supposed to take on some sort of leadership role and use this artifact to save her people? She might freak out from the power and damn them for all time.

Now she understood how Atlantis had become corrupt. They had lived isolated on their island kingdom in the middle of the Atlantic Ocean, equals at peace with one another. But then they started exploring and got in touch with regular humans. Those people had been far less advanced, with no special strength or speed and no individual powers. Of course the Atlanteans had started to feel superior. Instead of being humble and using their powers to raise up the rest of the world, they began to lord over it. A few Atlanteans never learned their lesson and had acted like that even after Atlantis was punished and sank into the sea. Mars Sans Pitié had been like that probably even before he found that artifact to magnify his power. Once he had it, he became a despot.

But what about her? She'd like to think she'd use her enhanced power wisely, but until a few months ago, she'd been nothing but an underachieving screwup. She'd been turning things around, and she felt herself growing every day, but had she grown enough? Even now, she was almost powerless, constantly on the run and being manipulated by forces she could barely understand. If, suddenly, she was the one in power, who knew how she would react?

"First things first." She sighed. "Let's get through this night alive, and then we can figure out what to do with that artifact."

As she boarded the truck with the Atlanteans and mercenaries, she began to make terrible calculations in her head. How many people would get hurt tonight? How many killed? Elaine could save a couple, but that was the limit of her strength. At least they had brought along a plentiful supply of the healing water, but in the firefight, would there even be a chance to give it to people in time to save them?

The scientists were probably right; it probably couldn't bring back the dead.

Jaxon sat on the hard wooden bench in the back of the truck and put her head in her hands.

She felt a soft touch on her shoulder. It was so dark in the back of the truck with the canvas awning blocking out the starlight, she didn't know who it was until Vivian spoke.

"It's okay to be scared, honey. We all are. Even these desert rebels who have been fighting all their life."

Jaxon blinked. Until Vivian said that, Jaxon hadn't realized that she had been worrying only about other people and not herself.

Now she did.

"Oh no," she moaned, shaking her head. She didn't want to die. She had never felt her life was worth much until all this craziness started to happen, but then she had finally found a place, a reason for living. She didn't want to lose that now.

The truck's motor ignited with a dull roar that sounded loud in the otherwise-silent desert. The Jeep ahead of them started up too. They headed out, headlights off, as Jaxon gripped Vivian's hand.

After a few minutes, they came out of the hills and swung to the west to get onto the track that led to the prison camp. Once they did, they turned on their headlights. Jaxon lifted up the bottom of the canvas awning and peeked out.

In the distance, the prison camp stood out like a beacon in the desert. Floodlights lit the interior and the surrounding area. Even though they were still a mile away, Jaxon could clearly make out the grim concrete barracks, the metal guard towers, the barbed-wire fence, and the large cluster of tents where her people led a miserable existence.

Suddenly, she realized she no longer felt afraid. The adrenaline had kicked in, and all she wanted was to get this done.

When they got within half a mile, the driver of the Jeep honked his horn several times. A tiny figure in one of the guard towers flanking the gate waved. She could hear the crackle of the radio in the truck's cab up front.

"Everything sounds okay," Vivian said. "They're welcoming us in, if my bad Arabic is getting that right. Put the awning down. It looks suspicious."

Jaxon did as she was told, but sitting in the back of the truck completely blind made her fidgety. She looked around at the rest of the team in the dim light. Everyone seemed on edge, even the Tuaregs.

This is a bad idea, she thought.

She peeked out from under the canvas again, but Vivian pulled her back. The mercenary pulled out her bowie knife.

"If you have to look out, do this."

Vivian poked a little hole in the canvas right next to Jaxon.

"Go ahead," Vivian said. "You'll be able to see out, but as dark as it is in here, they won't be able to see in."

Jaxon peeked out. They were just driving up to the gate, the Jeep in the lead. The gate did not open.

Instead, a man who looked like an officer flanked by a pair of machine-gun-toting soldiers came up to the other side of the gate, staring at them through the wire mesh.

The Jeep and truck parked. One of the Tuaregs, dressed in military uniform, got out and went up to the gate, holding up an identification card.

The officer looked at it a second before calling out to the tower. An electric motor hummed, and the gate slowly slid to the side.

The Tuareg hopped back in the Jeep, and the two vehicles moved forward again. Despite Vivian's reassurance, Jaxon moved away from the hole, not wanting the guards to spot her bright-blue Atlantean eyes.

The back of the truck lay open, and light from the gate shone on the back seats. The guards would see them soon enough. Everyone got their guns ready. The Tuaregs had taken all the places close to the opening so that the Atlanteans and white people would be hidden in the shadow.

The officer came around back, saying something in a friendly voice. Jaxon noticed an automatic pistol in a holster on his belt. The man hadn't drawn it or even kept his hand on it. He was obviously fooled for the moment. One of the Tuaregs a little farther in held up a cigarette. The officer said something that sounded like a thank-you and clambered in.

As soon as he got inside, Winston touched his shoulder.

"Shhh," the Englishman said. "Everything's all right."

The man froze.

"Sit down. Relax," Winston said in a voice that sounded as if he were coaxing a kitten out from under the couch. The officer sat next to him.

One of the Tuaregs giggled, an odd sound from a tough desert warrior.

"You have great magical, Sea Person," the Tuareg said in heavily accented English. "What you want me tell him to do?"

"Tell him I want—"

A series of explosions rocked the air. The entire truck shook, and Jaxon was jolted out of her seat.

The officer looked around, eyes growing wide.

Before Winston could stop him, he drew his pistol from his holster.

And then everything went wrong.

CHAPTER 10

AUGUST 27, THE SAHARA DESERT, A FEW
MILES EAST OF TIDJIKJA, MAURITANIA
11:30 P.M.

Winston tried to grab the gun from the officer's hand.
The pistol fired, and Winston flew backward with a
cry. Several other guns went off all at once. Jaxon
cringed on the floor where she fell. When she dared
to look again, she saw the officer dead and the
Tuaregs and mercenaries pouring from the back of
the truck. Elaine crouched over Winston. The
Englishman's shirt was soaked with blood.

"Wait!" Jaxon cried. "Save your energy. Use the
water instead."

"Good idea," the healer replied, grabbing the

nearest jug of water. "I don't want to be so tired I can't move."

A bullet popped through the canvas, opening up holes on either side of them and letting fingers of light in. Jaxon and Elaine crouched lower. Elaine put the jug to Winston's lips. The Englishman murmured something.

"Drink," Jaxon said.

Several bullets pinged off the front of the truck.

"*What if they hit the gas tank?*" Elaine shouted. "We have to get out of here!"

Winston had already downed a cupful or two of water. Jaxon grabbed him and hauled him out of the truck... and straight into a nightmare.

The Tuaregs were firing at the towers and at guards running across the open enclosure. Bullets came back at them from all directions. A line of bullets stitched up the sand inches from Jaxon's feet, forcing her to dive for cover under the truck, hauling Winston with her. Elaine did not follow.

Looking desperately around, she spotted her bending over a fallen Tuareg who had a gunshot to the shoulder.

More bullets pinged off the truck. She couldn't see who was firing at her. All she saw were the prone forms of those who had been hit and the running feet of those who still survived.

Then she saw something that made her heart grow cold.

Vivian lay on the ground about ten feet in front of the truck. She was not moving.

Then Jaxon saw she had a more immediate problem. She saw a trickle of gasoline running out of the truck's engine, making a puddle beneath the cab not five feet from where she and Winston lay.

The Englishman groaned.

"Can you move?" Jaxon asked.

A flurry of bullets clattered off the truck's cab, sending sparks dangerously close to the puddle of gasoline.

"I can move away from this!" Winston shouted and leapt out from under the truck, pulling her with him.

And they were back in the firestorm. She tore herself from Winston's grasp and sprinted to where Vivian lay.

Jaxon wailed. Her friend had been shot all over, her uniform a mass of blood. Several Tuareg warriors crouched close by, firing at the soldiers in the towers. She opened Vivian's mouth and poured some of the precious water down her throat then poured some more on every wound she could find.

A hot pain lanced through her calf. She looked down and saw a garish-red bullet wound. She poured some of the water on it, swallowed a mouthful, and felt a rush of cool relief. The pain departed instantly.

Jaxon poked a finger through the bullet hole in her uniform and found the skin had healed. A nearby Tuareg took a hit, and she ran to him, her legs feeling fine.

Another deafening explosion knocked her down before she could get halfway to him. The world went red. She fumbled the jug, sloshing out some of the liquid before she caught it. One of the buildings nearby, the one that looked like a lab on the satellite photo, erupted in flame. Jaxon remembered a brief glimpse she had caught of it in all the chaos when she had jumped out of the truck. It had been where the first explosions had gone up. And now another, more powerful detonation ripped the building apart, sending chunks of concrete in all directions.

Who was blowing up the lab? That hadn't been her side.

Jaxon regained her balance and hurried over to the Tuareg.

One of his companions knelt beside the body,

firing up at the tower. She recognized him as the one who spoke a bit of English. He glanced at Jaxon then at the man she was lifting up and said, "He gone to God."

"Not yet, he hasn't!" she shouted back over the roar of the man's assault rifle.

Again, she administered the water left over from Earth's creation. Within a second, the man opened his eyes and sat up. The English-speaking Tuareg gasped with surprise and looked at Jaxon with awe.

A clatter of bullets hitting the truck reminded Jaxon of why she was out here in the first place.

She pointed at the truck. "Get away from the truck! It's going to blow!"

Her words got drowned out by the gunfire, but her meaning was clear enough. The Tuaregs ran.

Then Jaxon remembered Vivian. She still lay a few feet from the truck, just now beginning to rise. Because of her terrible wounds, the water had taken longer with her.

Jaxon sprinted back to her, grabbed her under one arm, and ran toward the ruined lab that lay shrouded by a cloud of smoke.

I hope they're done blowing up that building. Otherwise, we're going to be stuck between two explosions.

An instant later, the truck lit up.

The force of the explosion threw Jaxon and Vivian several feet to land face-first in the pile of rubble. Jaxon smacked her head hard. The world spun, the sounds becoming muted. She could barely hear the battle over a painful ringing in her ears. Her lungs filled with smoke and grit, and her nose filled with the smell of burning.

After a minute, her head cleared. Blearily, she looked around, the scene hazy with the smoke still hanging over the building and the great column of black smoke billowing from the burning truck.

The first thing she noticed after that was Vivian reloading her gun.

The second thing she noticed was the jug of healing water. It lay on the ground, empty, its contents spilled on the desert sand.

Jaxon got onto her knees, trying to get her head together. Gunfire flashed through the smoke. Dimly, she could see one whole side of the barbed-wire fence off to her left rocking back and forth. Suddenly, with a metallic screech that tore through the ringing in her ears, a large section collapsed and fell to the ground with a crash. The fire from the towers in that direction intensified.

Closer to her, she saw men from both sides lying

on the ground, their bodies torn by the merciless bullets. She felt sorry for them all. None of this needed to happen.

A breeze wafted away some of the smoke, and she saw the Jeep standing untouched close to the flaming truck.

The Jeep! There were several jugs of healing water in the back!

"Cover me," Jaxon told Vivian.

She didn't wait to see if the mercenary heard her. She took off running, pushing her body to its utmost to get enough speed to make it through the fusillade alive.

None of the bullets touched her. She got to the Jeep in less than two seconds and grabbed a water jug in either hand.

The first person she came across was one of the prison guards. She poured some water into his mouth and on the gaping wound in his chest, kicked his gun out of reach, and ran to the next wounded man. This was a Tuareg. Within a second, she had administered the water, and she ran to the next patient. This time, it was a soldier and a rebel lying side by side, dying with the same look of terror on their faces. She helped them both.

A dim part of her mind heard loudspeakers

blaring an urgent message in Arabic from all the towers. She didn't understand it and didn't have time for it. She saw Elaine lying nearby, cradling her hand. A bullet had passed right through the palm. Jaxon healed it and moved on.

After helping out another wounded man, she noticed the gunfire slackening somewhat. She didn't know why and didn't have time to find out. Mateo lay not far off, his chest riddled with bullets. She poured the remains of one of the jugs all over him and moved on, having no idea whether he would live or not.

Some of the people she came across were beyond help. Guards and rebels alike had taken their last breath before she could get to them.

She picked up her speed, sweat pouring from her body, her lungs burning from the smoke and exertion, and she ran at blurring speed from one fallen person to another. She drained the second jug and ran back to the Jeep to get two more.

It was then that she realized the shooting had stopped entirely. That voice still blared from the loudspeakers. She was about to stop and look for Grunt or Vivian to ask what it meant when she noticed a prison guard with bullet wounds in both legs trying to crawl away. She ran to him. He looked at her, eyes wide with terror and pain, and pointed a pistol at her face. She kicked it out of his hand before he could pull the trigger and knelt down beside him.

She poured the water on one wound, slapped aside a punch aimed at her head, and poured some more water on the second wound. She left him staring in wonder at his legs, the pistol lying forgotten nearby.

After tending to three more wounded, she had no one left to heal, and she finally took a good look around her.

What she saw amazed her.

Firstly, everyone had stopped firing. The soldiers had backed off. The ones in the towers had ducked behind their protective metal walls and weren't showing themselves. The Tuaregs had hidden behind whatever cover they could and looked around warily.

The second thing she noticed was that the Atlanteans had broken free. Through the smoke, she could see they had torn down most of one wall of the prison camp. One of the towers had been nearly ripped from its foundations and leaned crazily to one side. Several prisoners lay on the ground, obviously shot by people in that same tower, but a couple of Atlanteans moved among them, pressing their hands against wounds. They were healers like Elaine.

Then she noticed the most remarkable thing of all. A man in an American general's uniform was walking toward them with his hands in the air. An older Mauritanian man in a business suit walked right behind him, holing a pistol to the general's head.

She spotted Vivian and Grunt not far off and ran to them.

"Is that General Meade?" she asked.

"No, it's not," Grunt replied. "I don't know who that is."

He sounded as confused as Jaxon felt.

The loudspeaker blared again, and the man with the gun to the general's head stopped and looked around nervously.

"What's that guy been saying?" Jaxon asked.

"He's the commander of the garrison, and he told his men to stop firing."

"Why? He was winning."

"I don't know."

The American general and the Mauritanian man approached.

"Salek!" one of the Tuaregs cried.

"What does that mean?" Jaxon asked.

"It's the name of their vice president," Vivian said.

"Yes, I am Vice President Salek," the man said in English. "And if you don't back off and let me go, I will kill your general."

Grunt shrugged. "Not my general. I'm done with generals. No more generals in my life. Shoot them all, if you ask me."

Vice President Salek looked confused, but his gun never wavered.

"You mean you didn't attack on the orders of General Corbin?"

Jaxon stepped forward. "No, we came to free the People of the Sea, my people."

"Quiet, girl," Salek said. "I'm talking to the man."

Grunt jabbed a thumb in Jaxon's direction. "She's in charge of this outfit, so you better get used to talking to her, buddy. Considering your situation, you don't get to be too choosy right now."

"So what's going on?" Jaxon demanded.

"This backstabber," Salek emphasized his point by pressing the pistol hard against the general's temple, "is General Corbin. He came here to buy our genetic information. Instead, his Atlantean bodyguard blew up the lab. Why? You could have bought it all! And now the Tuaregs are helping the People of the Sea. Why? And my own prison commandant turns against me and stops the battle when we are about to win. Why?"

Despite having a gun against his head, General Corbin smiled. "Careful, Mr. Vice President. All this worrying is going to give you a heart attack."

A hard-eyed officer strode through the haze, flanked by several guards. Judging from the snarl the vice president made when he noticed him, Jaxon figured this was the prison commandant. They exchanged some harsh words in Arabic.

"What's going on?" Jaxon asked.

"The prison commandant is telling Salek to give up," Vivian said. "Salek is saying no and threatening to kill the general if they don't let him go. If that happens, the US would probably invade, and that would be bad for everyone."

"Would Salek do that?"

"He sounds desperate enough. Now the prison commandant is saying that he doesn't want to imprison his own people and that they are free to go. The vice president says he'll be executed for treason."

"So who's this General Corbin guy?" Jaxon asked.

"I have no idea," Vivian admitted.

Grunt gave a shrug to show he didn't know either.

The argument went back and forth. Salek was surrounded by both soldiers and rebels, all pointing their guns at him, but he was not a man to be cowed. He knew they wouldn't dare shoot. If an American general lost his life here, the entire country would be in danger. Its vice president was perfectly happy to threaten his own country with the wrath of a foreign superpower in order to save his skin. It was quite obvious he wasn't bluffing.

Salek got his wish. He edged over to the Jeep that the Tuareg had captured, made General Corbin get in the driver's seat, and ordered him at gunpoint to drive out of the prison.

The Jeep roared out of the gate and soon became a dwindling pair of taillights far away in the night. Then the lights winked out. No doubt Salek had turned them off so they couldn't be followed.

"Well, that's one problem solved," Jaxon said.

Vivian shook her head. "No, honey. We haven't seen the last of them."

CHAPTER 11

AUGUST 27, THE SAHARA DESERT, A FEW MILES EAST OF TIDJIKJA, MAURITANIA MIDNIGHT

Jaxon walked through the ragged tents of the prison camp. Agerzam and some more Tuareg had driven up in a long column of trucks and were having peace talks with the prison commandant. The commandant's main preoccupation was to make sure he and his men didn't get punished for letting the People of the Sea go. Having a conscience had put them all in grave danger from the government.

Let those guys deal with it, Jaxon thought. Heavy sadness and unbearable weariness weighed her down. So much death. So much suffering. And for what? So the two strongest countries in the world could get a little stronger?

The prison camp looked like something out of a nightmare. Dirty and hungry Atlanteans lay listless in tents infested with fleas. There were only two toilets for several hundred people, and those stank like nothing she had ever smelled. Thick black clouds of flies swarmed over them. Several of the former prisoners tried to speak with her, but she could only shrug and reply in English that she didn't understand.

She didn't understand a lot of things. Like why the world had to be this way.

The prison guards had all fled this part of the compound. The towers stood empty and the gaping hole in the fence left unguarded. The Atlanteans milled around, unsure what to do next. It was too far to walk anywhere, and they all looked at the conference going on between the guards and the rebels, wondering what their fate would be.

A Tuareg with a video camera moved through the crowd, speaking to some of the prisoners. Jaxon went over to him.

"What are you doing?"

He looked confused, replying in his own language.

She pointed to the video camera.

"Internet," the rebel said. "Tuareg YouTube."

"Come film this," Jaxon said, leading him to the filthy toilets. The rebel wrinkled his nose and took a close-up panning shot. She wondered how many hits this video would get and if anyone would care or just move on to the next online distraction.

She left the Tuareg to do his job and went back to her friends.

What she found startled her.

General Corbin wasn't the only general here. In fact, there were four. Two were Mauritanian and were now prisoners of the prison commandant, who planned to use them as bargaining chips to protect himself and his men. The other general was American. He sat on the sand by the ruined laboratory with his hands tied behind his back while being interrogated by Vivian and Grunt. Vivian looked surreal. Her clothes were perforated with bullet holes and soaked with blood, and yet there she stood, completely fine.

"We got him!" Grunt said as Jaxon came up to them. "This is General Meade."

Vivian frowned. "Yeah, but there's something wrong with him."

Grunt let out a derisive laugh. "He's just shamming."

"Where's General Corbin?" Meade said. His uniform was torn, and he had several bruises on his face, but otherwise, he looked unhurt. "General Corbin left me and didn't tell me what to do."

"He's been saying that since we caught him," Vivian told her. "He didn't even put up any resistance."

"Where's General Corbin?" Meade asked again.

Jaxon knelt down beside him. "Why do you need him so much?"

"To know what to do."

Jaxon cocked her head. That didn't sound like a general talking.

Then she saw his eyes—lifeless, with no personality or spark.

She had seen eyes like that before.

On Brett, just before he tried to kill her in Timbuktu.

She glanced at his bonds. His hands were tied with thick rope.

"Get out of those ropes, and I'll take you to General Corbin."

With a single flex of his muscles, the middle-aged

man snapped the thick ropes as if they were made of rubber bands.

"Whoa!" Grunt shouted, jumping back and leveling his assault rifle.

"Hold on!" Jaxon said. "He's been changed, like Brett was. He's like a zombie. And since he hasn't been given any instructions, I don't think he's any danger to us."

"Yeah, right," Grunt said, keeping his gun at the ready.

"Are we going to see General Corbin?" Meade asked. "I need to know what to do. He didn't tell me what to do after helping Orion destroy the laboratory."

"Wait a minute," Jaxon told him. She had backed off even though he didn't seem dangerous at the moment. "Grunt, go get Winston. He'll get to the bottom of this."

Grunt refused to budge, so Vivian went and got him. A minute later, the Englishman faced General Meade.

"You just relax," Winston told him. "Relax and tell me everything that happened to you."

General Meade's eyes grew even more lifeless, and he began to speak.

What they heard blew their minds. General

Meade told them everything—about the Poseidon Project, about giving Dr. Yamazaki a stroke, about using the Grants to spy on Jaxon, about hunting for her once she escaped, about Orion, and then falling prey to General Corbin. The last thing he recalled clearly was being drugged and then waking up as one of the Poseidon Project's subjects.

His account grew vague after that. It was as if his mind remained detached from his actions. Since he had no willpower, what he did and what was done to him did not stick in his memory. In a few jumbled phrases, he mentioned physical training and hypnotism sessions and returning to his old job under Corbin's instructions. Then he came here with General Corbin and Orion.

Grunt let out a low whistle. "Damn, if it wasn't for all the stuff he made us do back in the day, I'd almost feel sorry for the guy."

"Where's Orion, that Atlantean you spoke of?" Jaxon asked. She didn't like the idea of one of Corbin's followers with Atlantean powers still running free.

General Meade shrugged.

"What does Orion look like?" Jaxon asked.

"Typical Atlantean skin and eye color. About

five feet, ten inches. Stocky build. Muscular. Dread-locks," the general said.

"That could be any of a hundred guys over there!" Grunt said, gesturing toward the compound. "What were Orion's instructions?"

"The same as mine. To blow up the lab," General Meade said. "We wired grenades we took off some guards we killed, plus some canisters of natural gas we found in the mess-hall kitchen, and detonated the lab."

"What were Orion's instructions after blowing up the lab?"

"The same as mine. To report back to General Corbin. Where is he? Can I go to him now?"

"In a minute," Jaxon said. "And did you report back to him?"

"The attack happened before we could make it to the general. We got in a fight with more guards and got split up. I don't know what happened to Orion after that."

Jaxon looked around the camp nervously. Where could he be?

"Does Orion speak Arabic?" she asked the general.

"No."

"Well, then he shouldn't be too hard to find,"

Jaxon said. "All we need to do is check on every young man with dreadlocks."

Jaxon and Grunt took one of the Tuaregs who could speak both Arabic and English and went around the camp, checking on all likely candidates. After an hour of searching, they didn't come up with anyone.

By the time they made it back, frustrated and wondering where Orion could have disappeared to, the prison commandant and Agerzam had come to an agreement. The Tuareg would withdraw, taking the Atlanteans with them. The prison commandant would not surrender or give up any weapons, so the government would have a harder time accusing them of treason. The Tuaregs could take the water trucks and food for the Atlanteans. The commandant would keep the two Mauritanian generals, however, as extra insurance. In the meantime, the Tuaregs would publicize what had happened here on the chance that they'd get some international sympathy.

No one held out much hope for that, though.

"We are a poor corner of the world with no oil and no mineral riches," Agerzam said. "We have been trying to get attention for our plight for years with no success."

It was now approaching dawn, and everyone felt

dead tired. Wearily, they helped the Atlanteans board the trucks, buried their dead, and headed off into the desert. Everyone had a long drive ahead of them. The trucks would all split up and get as much distance between them and the camp as possible. They knew the army would be coming after them soon enough.

Jaxon nodded off in the front of a truck driven by Vivian, the back crammed with Atlanteans. She knew she should be planning their next move, but she felt sick to her stomach from all the violence. Every time she glanced at Vivian, who still wore her bloodstained clothes, she felt like throwing up.

At last, she fell asleep, only to have frightening, rapid-fire dreams of fire and blood and of fingers clenching tight around her neck.

When she woke with a start a couple of hours later, the sun was already a few degrees above the horizon. Craning her neck out the window, she looked behind her and saw the two Land Rovers behind their truck, plus a few of the Tuareg vehicles. It was only a tenth of the vehicles that had been part of the attack and rescue mission. She presumed the others had spread out to other areas of the desert. She lay back in the seat and tried to doze. She knew she'd need to conserve her strength for what was to come. This fight wasn't over by a long way.

After another hour, they parked behind some dunes and draped all the vehicles with light-brown tarps the same color as the desert. Their vehicles still cast a telltale shadow, but hopefully, any air reconnaissance would think they were sand dunes.

Jaxon got out and stretched her legs in the blazing heat. She desperately needed a bath and a good, long sleep. She knew neither of those things would happen today. The Tuaregs and refugees set up a camp away from the vehicles. Jaxon remembered the precautions Grunt and Vivian had always taken when they first crossed the Sahara to camp away from the Land Rovers in case of an air strike.

Jaxon shook her head. It would be nice to be in a life in which she didn't have to worry about air strikes or Russian agents or her own government, but she hadn't had a life like that in a long time. She had almost forgotten what it was like.

She noticed that while the Tuareg tents and their own tents were camouflaged, the refugees' tents were not. They were made of any old bits of canvas or plastic sheeting and came in all colors. They stood out against the dull shades of the desert. The

Tuaregs and her own people camped away from the refugees.

Great, she thought. *Leaving them on their own in case of an air strike.*

While it was a callous thing to do, she couldn't fault the logic. There was no point in all getting blown up together.

Once camp was set up and everyone had eaten a cold meal, the Atlantis Allegiance and Atlantis Guard got together and spent much of the day trying to interrogate General Meade. They didn't learn much of value. The man was half zombie.

He did come out with one weird detail, though.

"We need to make an army of Atlanteans to protect us against a new threat," General Meade said. "Aliens are planning to invade the Earth. There have been more and more UFOs flying in the upper atmosphere, generally over military installations and nuclear power plants. The UFO that crashed at Roswell even had an inscription of Atlantean DNA."

That got her team into a huddle.

"This is amazing!" Otto said. "A leading general actually admitting that UFOs exist. But what could they want with the Atlanteans?"

"Don't believe it for a minute, pyro," Grunt said.

"Edward talked to me about this once a while back. It's all fake."

Jaxon's stomach turned when she heard Edward's name. The hacker had been killed for his association with the Atlantis Allegiance. Killed for helping her.

Make this mean something. Those had been his last words to her.

"How did he know it was fake?" Otto asked.

"Not sure. He spouted a bunch of technobabble. You know how he was. But if he didn't believe in it, I don't believe in it."

Jaxon considered this. "Edward believed in a lot of conspiracy theories. If he didn't believe in that one, maybe it wasn't true."

"What do you mean?" Otto said. "We're living in a conspiracy theory. Secret government projects, a lost continent, supernatural powers... you even talked to Edward after he died."

"Just because one conspiracy is true doesn't mean they're all true," Dr. Yamazaki said. "And the Atlantean powers do have a scientific explanation. We just haven't had time to study them yet."

She paused, looking as if she wanted to say more, then glanced at Jaxon and stopped talking.

That's right, Jaxon thought. *I remember you*

doubted me when I said I saw Edward. I don't want to have that argument again.

"So now what?" Elaine asked. "Do we just ignore this?"

Grunt shook his head. "I'm not sure what to do about this. Someone high up was faking this UFO stuff and managed to fool General Meade. I remember Meade always did believe in UFOs. A lot of the officers and men joked about it behind his back, although some believed in them too. Made for some interesting arguments in the mess hall."

"Maybe that other general did it. The one the politician took away." Jaxon said.

Grunt shrugged. "Maybe. It's hard to tell, being stuck out here. We're working blind now that Edward's gone."

"But why fake a bunch of UFO sightings?" Otto asked. "That doesn't make any sense."

"Maybe to manipulate this general here," Mateo said. "This other guy, General Corbin, he's the real puppet master, just like Jaxon suggested. He's been leading Meade on and making him do his dirty work while he hides in the shadows. You said maybe this Atlantean army was being made as a private force in order to stage a coup in the United States."

"The American people wouldn't stand for it," Otto told the Peruvian.

"They would if they were scared," Mateo replied.

"Scared of a UFO invasion? Come on," Otto replied.

Mateo shrugged. "Why not? Half the population believes in them already. There are even UFO cults that try to contact aliens. There are some in my country, and I've heard there are some in the United States too."

"It just seems a bit too far-fetched to make people accept a coup," Otto said.

"General Corbin is probably working slowly, adding more and more UFO reports to the news and getting people riled up," Grunt said.

Otto scratched his head. "Come to think of it, there have been more UFOs in the news lately. Some pretty cool sightings. Some looked pretty real."

"Or well-faked," Mateo said.

Jaxon shook her head. "The real question is, what is Corbin going to do next?"

No one had an answer to that.

And so the meeting broke up with them having more questions than answers.

The day dragged on. They had decided not to

travel during the daytime because the dust plumes kicked up by even a few vehicles were visible for miles. There was nothing to do and not enough water to wash. A gritty wind picked up and made Jaxon's eyes itch and put a bitter taste in her mouth. The children cried.

All through the day, Tuareg warriors came up to her and Elaine to thank them for healing them. One even bragged that he had been shot, healed by Elaine, then got shot again and healed by Jaxon and what he called her "magic water."

"We're getting quite a reputation here," Jaxon told the Atlantean healer.

"A bit too much of one," Elaine replied, looking worried. "I don't really want everyone spreading around the idea that the People of the Sea have all these powers."

"I don't see how we can stop it after what we did at the battle. And did you see the prisoners? They tore open the fence and knocked over a tower with their bare hands."

Elaine made a face. "We've always survived by being anonymous."

"Yeah, and we've always been on the run and persecuted. Maybe it's time for another strategy."

Winston turned to her. "You're right that we're

always running, always hiding, and while that hasn't secured our rights, we've survived, haven't we? How many other ancient civilizations are still around after all this time? Do you know any Canaanites? Or Aztecs? Have you ever met a Sassanid? We predate all these civilizations, and we've outlived them all."

Jaxon didn't reply. What they said made sense. It didn't sit well with her, though. It seemed too much like giving in to bullying, and she had done that for far too long in her life.

Funny how all those schoolyard bullies who had tormented her, all those rich girls who called her names and laughed at her not having any parents, how petty they seemed now. Their perfect hair and fashionable clothes wouldn't count for anything out here in the desert or in a fight with Russian agents. Nothing they could say could touch her now. If she met someone like that, she would just laugh in their face.

No, she faced bigger bullies these days.

When night fell, the camp prepared to move out. They drove a long time through the night, Jaxon not knowing where. Occasionally, the crackle of the radio broke the silence of the Land Rover as other groups called in with coded updates.

They stopped before sunrise, and Vivian and

Jaxon gratefully pitched their tent and lay down in their sleeping bags, hoping to catch a few hours of rest before the broiling sun made it too hot to sleep.

She immediately plunged into the dream world, catching fragments of visions of Timbuktu and the people she knew there and of the alleys of Marrakech. Edward's plump face appeared before her. He seemed worried, his mouth working as if shouting something at her, and yet she heard no sound.

What? her sleeping mind asked her dead friend. *What are you trying to tell me?*

Then there came a sound but not from Edward's lips.

It was the dull thud of flesh hitting flesh right beside her. She struggled to awaken.

A firm hand clamped on her mouth.

CHAPTER 12

AUGUST 28, THE SAHARA DESERT, ON THE OUTSKIRTS OF NOUAKCHOTT, MAURITANIA

5:30 A.M.

The sun was just rising over the desert, turning the sands to gold, when General Corbin made his move. They had driven all night, Vice President Salek sitting in the passenger seat and covering him with a pistol, giving him directions to the capital, Nouakchott, some two hundred fifty miles away. Corbin was surprised they didn't go to the town of Tidjikja, which was so much closer, but maybe there weren't enough troops there to help him. Or maybe he didn't trust them since their neighbors at the prison camp had just turned on the government. Or maybe Salek just wanted to get as far away from the Tuaregs as possible.

Corbin allowed himself to remain a prisoner. Salek was easier to handle if he thought he was in charge, and besides, the guy knew the way, and Corbin didn't. But as the sun came up in the east and they got onto a well-driven desert track and the smoke fires from the outlying areas of Nouakchott appeared on the horizon, Corbin slammed on the brakes. Salek lurched forward, hitting the dashboard. Corbin grabbed the politician's gun while he was still stunned and turned it on him.

"This is where you get out, Mr. Vice President."

Salek looked around at the bleak desert. There wasn't a vehicle in sight. Corbin handed him a canteen.

"We passed a village about ten miles back. You can make it. Get out."

Salek reluctantly stepped out of the Jeep, his expensive leather shoes crunching on the sand.

"You leave me in the middle of the desert?"

Corbin smiled. "You'll make it. You're a survivor. You'll get some killer blisters, walking all that way in those fancy shoes, though."

Corbin stepped on the gas and left the corrupt politician in the dust.

After he had stopped laughing, Corbin considered his options and his resources. This Jeep looked in good repair, and he had spare jerricans of fuel in the back. He could drive all day and well into the night. The problem was that the Jeep had military markings, and seeing a white man in an American uniform driving it would raise uncomfortable questions wherever he went. Besides the suspicious Jeep, he had a 9mm automatic pistol with eight rounds of ammunition, a box of flares, and enough water for a day. He was safe for the moment. Some food would be nice. He had plenty of local currency in his pocket and some American dollars as well, but he didn't want to go into any towns with this Jeep. Every settlement of any decent size had troops in it.

So where should he go? He needed to avoid towns as much as possible and get back into contact with Isadore and the McKay twins, but they were all the way down in Mali, and he no longer had his satellite phone. Even worse, if he didn't check in with the Pentagon pretty soon, they were going to wonder if he had disappeared. It wouldn't take long for the local CIA office to hear about the fighting at the prison camp, and they'd put two and two together. His own government trying to save him might ruin all his plans.

Might? No, *would* ruin his plans. There was no way they weren't going to hear of this and go looking for him and General Meade, and when they did, they would start asking uncomfortable questions about what he was doing here. The damage had been done. It was time for damage control.

General Corbin did a hard U-turn and headed back toward the capital. He drove as fast as the rough track would allow. He had to get somewhere safe before Salek managed to spread the word.

Briefly, he wondered what had happened to Dimitri and Nadya. He hadn't seen them when he was planning the lab explosion or trying to survive the attack. Had they been captured? That could be a problem. They knew enough about his plans to cause some real trouble.

But would they? And did they even know that he was working without the knowledge or permission of the US government?

He sped up. The sooner he got to civilization, the better.

As he drove, he noticed a smile had come to his lips. He even allowed himself to whistle a happy tune. It felt refreshing being out here in the warm early morning. The problem with getting promoted to a high level of command was that you never got to go into the field anymore. Your subordinates did all the fun stuff. General Meade had complained about the same thing before Corbin enslaved him.

Then he started to wonder what had happened to his two slaves. Meade might or might not have survived. He had no doubt that Orion had survived. If Meade had made it through the night, he was now a prisoner. That was too bad, but Corbin wasn't particularly worried. Meade wouldn't be able to tell the Atlantis Allegiance or the Mauritanians anything of value that they didn't already know. The real danger was if he fell into the hands of the CIA. That would be a disaster. He'd need to be taken care of before that.

Orion was a wild card. Right at the start of this trip, General Corbin had left him with simple instructions—capture Jaxon, and if that wasn't possible, kill her. Orion would be out there somewhere, awaiting his chance. He was much more awake than Meade and much more resourceful. While Orion had been drugged and hypnotized and experimented on, his mind had remained far more intact because he had been an Atlantean in the first place. He hadn't been through the dulling effect of the serum Dr. Jones had created. The human subjects, while developing some impressive abilities, were simply too brain-dead to function independently. Corbin had to prompt Meade every morning before Meade went to work and endure countless phones calls about simple decisions.

Corbin could see the outskirts of Nouakchott now. He could smell the salty tang in the sea breeze blowing in off the Atlantic, tinged with the pollution emitted by the city's one million inhabitants. Soon, the first houses appeared—low concrete buildings in dusty lots. Herds of sheep and goats nibbled on the sparse grass. He passed a gas station with a line of trucks waiting to fill up. The traffic began to pick up, and the road turned from a dirty track into a paved highway.

Corbin got ready. He would be stopped any moment now. On his way out of the city a couple of days ago, he had noticed several police checkpoints. Mostly, they just waved everyone through, but a Westerner in a military uniform, driving a Mauri-tanian Army Jeep, would not get the same courtesy. He had to keep cool.

A few minutes later, a policeman waved him to a stop.

General Corbin parked next to the two police cars sitting by the side of the road and got out with his hands plainly visible. He left his pistol under the driver's seat.

The police officers looked more confused than suspicious and, after some unsuccessful attempts to speak with him in French and Arabic, called in a commander who spoke English. General Corbin tried to look anxious and exhausted, not difficult considering the night he had been through.

He was in luck. The police commander had heard of his arrival in the country on a "diplomatic" mission, and he had heard a vague initial report of the attack on the prison, so he was prepared to believe Corbin's story when he said he had been on a state visit and went with Vice President Salek to visit a camp where the captured "terrorists" were kept. He explained that the Tuaregs had attacked the camp to free the terrorists, and he had escaped. The police commander looked like a conservative guy, with a permanent scowl and a look of intolerance. He probably mistrusted the People of the Sea for being different even before the government ordered them rounded up. It was easy to play on people's fears and prejudices.

The police commander radioed in to someone and began speaking in Arabic. Corbin tensed. If Salek had gotten back in time to spread his side of the story, he was in deep trouble.

But when the commander turned back to him, he looked at Corbin with concern and sympathy, not distrust.

"I have asked some more about the attack. Our vice president is still missing. My superior is very glad to hear you are alive. I am sad to say that we have not heard what happened to General Meade."

The police commander did not mention Orion. Perhaps being one of the People of the Sea, he was beneath the policeman's notice.

Corbin affected concern. "That's too bad. I lost sight of him during the fight. I suspect either he was killed, or the Tuaregs captured him."

The commander straightened. "I swear we will do all in our power to ensure his safe return."

"What's being done to find Vice President Salek?" Corbin wondered if he had died in the desert after all, but he doubted it. That guy couldn't be knocked off so easily.

"All the troops in the region have been mobilized. There have been a couple of skirmishes with the Tuaregs, and that is slowing down the search, but a major force left here a couple of hours ago."

Corbin nodded. Considering how far outside of town he had left Salek, he might only be getting access to a phone right now. Time was of the essence. If Salek called in while he stood here chatting to the police, he'd be behind bars before breakfast.

"I need to get to my embassy and speak with my government," Corbin said.

"Of course. I will take you there myself."

That wasn't the answer Corbin wanted, but he could think of no way to say no.

They hopped in a police cruiser with another officer and sped off through the streets of the capital. The city was spread out, with mostly one-story buildings and many empty lots, land being cheap in the desert. It took time to get to the embassy. Corbin felt tense the entire way, especially whenever the radio crackled to life, and yet he also felt incredibly alive. It was good to be at the center of the action for a change instead of commanding it from afar. He told himself he should savor these moments. Once he ruled the United States, he wouldn't get any more of them.

Every time the radio spoke with some message in

Arabic, he wondered if that was the message that would turn the car around and make it head for the nearest jail instead of the embassy, but his luck held. They came to a large compound surrounded by a high, smooth concrete wall. From a corner tower flew an American flag. Four marines guarded a steel gate. General Corbin leaped out of the car, thanked the police officers, and strode up to the marines. When they saw the general's stars on his dusty uniform, they snapped a salute.

Within a minute, he was in the embassy, which meant he was on US soil. Salek could call all he wanted now, and the Mauritanians couldn't touch him.

The Americans could, though.

⬚

Clifford Owen was the head of CIA operations in Mauritania. He was a middle-aged man who wore a conservative suit, spoke with a quiet voice, and had eyes that missed nothing. He kept a poker face as he sat behind his tidy desk in his large office in the embassy. Owen had a secretary fetch some breakfast for this general who had shown up unannounced on his doorstep, and Corbin dug in gratefully.

Corbin stayed on his guard, though. Owen was studying him as if he were some sample under a microscope.

"It's a pity the ambassador is away in Dakar for a conference," Owen said. "He's been notified and is taking the first plane back."

"Good," Corbin said, although he actually meant that it was good that he was away, not that he was heading back.

"Could you tell me what happened?"

Corbin repeated the story he had given the police commander, which was accurate as far as it went. Owen listened without saying a word and then asked a few more details about General Meade and his last known location. Then he asked the question he really wanted to know the answer to.

"General Corbin, I'm a bit unclear as to the nature of your mission here."

Here we go.

"That's classified."

"Surely you must know that I'm privy to any classified material relating to events in Mauritania."

"That's true, and you'll see the full report once it's written up."

"The reason I ask, sir, is because it seems strange that General Meade came here without his usual staff, in the company of a civilian who does not have security clearance, and with another general who does not have this region under his responsibility."

"I understand it might look strange, Mr. Owen, but this is a very specialized mission. We are liaising with the Mauritanian government regarding a new terror organization being organized among the ethnic group called the People of the Sea."

"I've heard of them," Owen said with a nod.

"The civilian is an American who originates from this ethnic group and is an expert on their culture. He was brought in as a consultant. I was brought in for my expertise in counterinsurgency and also because I, too, have some knowledge of this ethnic group. They have an interesting history, and studying them has been a hobby of mine for several years."

Owen's face remained a mask. "That should be in your CV."

"It wasn't relevant until now, but I will certainly add it."

"General Corbin, an American officer and an American civilian are missing in a terrorist attack, most likely either dead or captured. I've already been on the phone with the president."

Corbin shifted in his seat. Of course the president of the United States had been informed. This would hit international headlines within the hour if it hadn't already.

Owen must have anticipated his thoughts, because he said, "We're keeping this out of the press for the time being. Our Mauritanian allies are giving us their full cooperation. The last thing we need is a bunch of reporters sniffing around. But we can't keep it out of the press for long. What if the Tuaregs or this new terror group decide to put Meade or the civilian in a video? What if the press hears about their capture from YouTube before they hear about it from us?"

"That would be a disaster," Corbin conceded. *More for me than you,* he thought.

"So tell me more about this mission," the CIA official said. It came out like an order.

Corbin made a mental note to get rid of this guy once he took over.

"As I told you, that's classified. You'll get a full report when the mission is complete."

"I'm afraid that's not good enough, not after what happened last night."

Corbin thought for a moment and decided part of the truth would be better than none. "We have reason to believe these People of the Sea have established a network not only in the region, but with fellow members of their ethnic group in Europe, North America, and other countries. They think of themselves as special, the original race. They do have an ancient history in this region and may really predate all the other civilizations here. Some of the Arabs and Tuaregs and black Africans believe their stories. Some even believe they have magical powers. The People of the Sea have created a terrorist group that plans nothing less than world domination."

Owen scoffed. "The last time a terror group thought that, they got wiped off the map. It acted so arrogantly that every faction that could have become their allies ended up fighting against them."

"These groups are bound to fail, but they cause a hell of a lot of trouble in the meantime."

Owen nodded, and by the serious expression on his face, Corbin knew he had him. This man, like everyone in the CIA, had been trained for years to see the world as nothing but a series of threats. It was easy to play upon that preconception and turn it to his own purposes. Owen and Corbin spent an hour making preliminary plans about how to deal with the "terror" group. Corbin resisted the urge to fidget. Every minute that slipped by increased the chance of his being caught. But he had to placate this officer.

With the ambassador away, Owen was essentially in charge. He was by far the most dangerous person here as far as Corbin was concerned.

At last, he earned enough of Owen's confidence to get where he needed to be—in a soundproof room with a secure satellite telephone. That Owen guy was a real hard case. Not only did he ask all the right questions, but Corbin couldn't tell how much of his phony story the CIA agent believed. That planning session had just been a contingency in case Corbin had told the truth. It wouldn't be long before Owen did some checking up on him. Corbin had covered his tracks well, but it was difficult to hide something as big as the Poseidon Project. He needed to make this call and get out of there somehow.

Then inspiration struck.

He called Isadore. Thankfully, she actually picked up. Until that moment, Corbin hadn't been entirely sure she was still alive. He filled her in on the situation.

"This is bad. What do you want me to do?" his best assassin asked.

"Where are you now?"

"Crossing the border. We stole a vehicle from Doctors Without Borders. We can get to you within twenty-four hours."

"Good." He pulled out his cell phone, thanking himself for having the foresight to get a Mauritanian SIM card, and gave her his local number. "Call me on that line as soon as you get into town."

"What do you have planned?"

General Corbin smiled. "You're going to kidnap me."

CHAPTER 13

AUGUST 29, SOMEWHERE IN THE
SAHARA DESERT
6:00 A.M.

Jaxon had given up trying to struggle. She had fought
back in the tent and had been quickly knocked out.
When she had come to and discovered she was being
carried through the desert by an Atlantean man
running at least fifty miles per hour, she had put up a
fight, only to get knocked out again.

Now, as the sun rose on another punishing day
in the Sahara, she was being carried like a football
over sand dunes, still at that same impossibly fast and
steady pace. Her arms were pinned to her sides, and

she hung limp, the bouncing of Orion's running making her sore and dizzy.

He hadn't said a word. After a while, she had given up trying to talk. Every now and then, Orion would look at a compass, scan the horizon, and keep on running.

The sun rose higher. Jaxon began to sweat. How long could this guy keep it up? She had strength and endurance well beyond regular human levels, but Orion made her look like a wimp. She bet even Mateo couldn't match him.

She worried about Vivian. Orion had knocked her out before kidnapping Jaxon. Had he hit her hard enough to kill her? If not, had Elaine been able to heal her in time?

Jaxon kept craning her neck to look at the brilliant-blue sky, hoping to see Elaine's drone following them, but she saw nothing.

At last, Orion stopped, unceremoniously dumping Jaxon on the ground. She lay there, afraid to rise.

"I've been instructed to capture you," Orion told her, "but if you resist or it looks like I can't keep you until I get where we're going, I've been instructed to kill you."

Jaxon suppressed a shudder. "And where are we going?"

Instead of answering, he took a canteen hanging by a strap from his shoulder and handed it to her. He carried two canteens. She hoped they were both full.

"Drink."

She took several big gulps. The sun beat down on them now. Neither of them had a hat, although Jaxon did have a scarf she had wrapped around her head. She usually slept with it on to keep the sand out of her hair. It would be some measure of protection against the sun.

Orion took the canteen back and replaced the cap.

"Aren't you drinking?" Jaxon asked.

"I don't need it."

"Look, just let me go. General Meade is gone. He's probably dead or captured by the Tuareg rebels or something. You're free."

"I don't follow General Meade anymore. I follow General Corbin."

"That other guy? He got captured by the vice president. He's a prisoner. You're free!"

Orion picked her up.

"You don't have to do this!" Jaxon shouted. "We

can take you to my friends. I know scientists and Atlantean healers. They can help you."

"Remember what I said. Don't struggle."

Orion set off across the desert once more. Jaxon tried to relax, saving her energy and biding her time.

After a few miles, Jaxon felt a strange force pulling her attention ahead of them and a little to the east. She looked in that direction but saw nothing but the same searing desert. Orion kept going, but after a minute, he glanced in that direction too. His pace slowed. Jaxon felt that whatever was there, they had gotten closer to it.

Orion stopped, staring in the exact direction from which she felt the pull.

Oh no. He feels it too.

Orion got a puzzled look on his face. He set her down and stared. "There's something over there. How do I know that?" He motioned for her to follow. "Come. If you run, I'll chase you down and kill you."

She followed.

At first, they didn't see anything, but as the sensation grew stronger, Jaxon began to notice low mounds in the sand. Vaguely, she could make out square and rectangular shapes, and a clear area in the center. It looked like the village at the well but far more eroded. She was surprised that, sitting out here, exposed to the desert winds for all those millennia, there was anything left of the old settlement at all.

Orion looked around, his eyes not focusing on the ruins.

"It's the remains of one of our villages," Jaxon explained. "One of the villages for our people back when the desert was green. Look."

She kicked away sand on one of the mounds until she revealed two stone blocks, one standing on the other. Orion stared at them.

"We used to be traders and teachers. We helped found civilizations all over the world."

"Who's 'we'?" Orion asked.

"Our people, the descendants of the survivors of the fall of Atlantis."

Orion stared at her, his face blank. Jaxon had thought that this revelation would get some sort of reaction from him.

"Didn't you know any of this before?" Jaxon asked.

"No."

"Did you know your parents?"

"I was raised in CPS."

"Don't you want to know where you're from? What our people have been doing all this time?"

"I want to do my mission," Orion said, his voice

still flat. He looked around, a spark of curiosity finally appearing in his eyes.

For some reason, that gave Jaxon hope. It made him look more human.

"I also want to know why I sensed this place. I sensed you too. I couldn't see a thing in that camp last night, and yet I was drawn right to you. I can feel you standing there even when my back is turned. So don't try to run. I can track you down."

Jaxon looked out over the landscape, her eyes in a constant squint because of the sun's harsh glare on the sand. Where could she go? The desert made her a prisoner just as much as Orion did.

Orion headed to the other side of the ruins.

"There's something over here. Why can I feel that?" He sounded confused.

Jaxon felt it too. Something lay buried in that mound over there, the one surrounded by several smaller mounds.

They walked through the once-thriving town, some way station in a vast trade network, perhaps, but now reduced to nothing but a series of little sand dunes in the middle of nowhere. No wonder generations of archaeologists had missed places like these. Without her extra senses, she would never have found it.

Orion would never have found it either.

He's a Keeper of the Texts, just like me, she realized. *That makes him ten times as dangerous.*

They came to the mound. It looked like a large rectangular building and reminded her of the place where they had found the pendant. It hung around her neck right now. Luckily, it remained hidden beneath her blouse and the headscarf she wore around her head and neck.

Good thing I wore the headscarf to bed. Otherwise, this sun would have knocked me out by now.

Her throat had become dry again, and she felt the beginnings of a headache. She eyed the two canteens dangling on straps around Orion's shoulder. She had drunk probably a third of one. Was the other full? It was probably only nine in the morning. How were they going to survive all day out here?

The terrible memory of her and Vivian dying out in the desert came back to her. They had only survived by a miracle. She couldn't rely on a second one to save her.

Orion started digging with his bare hands at one end of the building. Despite her fear and the heat pressing down on her throbbing head, she knelt down by him and helped. As they cleared the sand, they began to uncover an altar similar to the one she and her friends had found in the last place, although a little smaller. The stone platform measured about six feet wide and four feet deep, set against the wall. Jaxon studied the remains of the wall behind it for a carved picture, but like in the last one, the desert winds had scoured away whatever message might have been there.

She spotted a seam around one of the altar stones.

"Here!" she said, not able to contain her excitement.

Orion tried to get a grip on the edge, but the space was too narrow. He searched around for a stone and bashed at the edge, breaking off hunks of the altar stone. Jaxon backed off as fragments flew all around.

"Watch it!" Jaxon shouted. "You'll break whatever's inside."

Orion ignored her. The stone shattered in his hands, and he got a bigger one, some fragment of an old building. It must have weighed fifty pounds, but he lifted it as though it were made of Styrofoam.

He brought it down on the altar stone with a loud crack. Both it and the altar stone broke into half a dozen pieces.

"You're smashing your own history!" Jaxon objected.

Orion still ignored her. He tossed the fragments over his shoulder one by one. Curiosity overruled Jaxon's anger, and she peered inside.

Like in the last place, a small cist lay beneath the altar stone, and in it, she saw the gleam of gold.

Orion lifted out a tablet about the size of a cutting board. It caught the sun, and Jaxon had to turn away from the glare. When he set it in his own shadow, Jaxon looked again.

The tablet was covered with writing—a strange, angular script that looked unlike anything Jaxon had ever seen in her travels. One corner was dented, the writing distorted.

"Good job, idiot," Jaxon said. "This thing has survived for who knows how many thousands of years, and you crush it."

"It's still legible," Orion said.

"Can you read it?"

"No. I suppose it's some ancient language. I took some archaeology classes in college. I don't recognize this. Probably some previously unknown language."

"Yeah, our language. Our heritage. Doesn't this move you at all?"

Orion shrugged. "Why should it?"

Jaxon rolled her eyes. What a loser. How couldn't you care about your past?

On the other hand, Jaxon realized, until all this craziness began, she didn't care about her own past either. She didn't care about anything at all. And she didn't have being hypnotized by a secret government project to use as an excuse.

Orion dropped it back in the cist.

"What are you doing?" Jaxon asked.

"We don't need it."

"It's important!" Jaxon couldn't bear letting it be lost again, even if it did end up in the wrong hands. Every link to their vanished civilization was precious.

"My mission is to take you to General Corbin, not dig around old ruins. I shouldn't have gotten distracted."

Jaxon had an idea. "But you did. You felt its pull. That's because you're Atlantean. You have a connection to it, and to me, and to all those people you've been fighting. That's more important than being a slave to Corbin."

Orion's face clouded with confusion for a moment, then he shook his head.

"Let's go. It will be easier if I carry you piggyback."

"At least let me take the tablet," Jaxon said, reaching for it.

As she bent over it, the world spun. She fell hard on her knees, her vision momentarily going dark. The fear and fatigue of the last few days, the discomfort of her sleepless night, and the heat beating down on her had become too much to bear.

Orion knelt beside her and gave her one of the canteens.

"Drink."

She drained it.

"I don't know how you can have run all this way without getting thirsty," she said.

"I am thirsty, but I can take it better than you can, than anyone can. There's a limit, though. We need to get going. We need to find a settlement before noon."

Jaxon grabbed the tablet.

"We don't need that," Orion said.

"I'm not leaving without it."

Orion put his hands around her throat. Jaxon tensed. He could crush her windpipe like she could bend a soda straw.

"Toss it," he ordered. "We don't need it."

"Yes, we do need it. Look, General Corbin prefers me alive, right? Well, I'm not leaving without this. Kill me if you want. And besides, he'll want any artifact from Atlantis. You can feel its power."

Orion thought for a moment as Jaxon's heart pounded in her chest. She hadn't meant it when she said she'd rather die than leave it behind. Maybe that reflected badly on her, but she preferred to live. She hadn't really cared about her life one way or the other until she had discovered her heritage. Now, what had once seemed like a burden felt more precious than anything in the world.

Orion removed his hands. "Very well. Get on my back and carry the tablet. If you try anything, you die. Even if you smash that tablet on my head as hard as you can, you'll only stun me for a moment or two. After that, I'll chase you down and kill you."

Jaxon nodded. She knew she could only push him so far.

She got on his broad back, feeling strangely childlike, and Orion checked his compass and started to run across the desert as fast as a Land Rover.

CHAPTER 14

AUGUST 29, SOMEWHERE IN THE SAHARA DESERT, MAURITANIA
11:00 A.M.

The hours and miles seemed to stretch out forever. The rhythmic bouncing of Orion's steady gait lulled Jaxon into a hazy half sleep. The sun had risen high, turning the desert into an oven. The metal tablet grew too hot to touch, and Jaxon had to wrap it in her headscarf, exposing her even more to the sun's punishing rays.

Through bleary eyes, she saw nothing, nothing but an endless plain of sand and stone, blinding in the sun's glare. Her throat and tongue had swollen, making speech difficult. Orion had only given her a little water. As the day grew hotter, he started drinking some himself. Sweat glistened off the dark skin of his shoulders and neck. Jaxon thought he had begun to slow down, but she couldn't be sure.

She couldn't be sure of anything except that she was helpless now. Her thoughts had become muddled, and she couldn't think of a plan to escape or even resist. Nor should she. If she managed to get away from Orion, she would die in this desert.

At times, she faded away, her vision darkening and her body slumping over Orion's shoulders. At some point, she couldn't remember when, he had started carrying the golden tablet.

It was during one of these periods of semiconsciousness that she got startled awake by a hoarse cry from her captor. She opened her eyes and immediately saw why he had cried out. A cluster of palm trees stood in the distance. They had found an oasis!

Orion sped up. As they approached, she spotted several tents pitched in the shade. Distant figures pointed and called to each other at their approach.

Despite being half dead with thirst, she couldn't help but smile to think of what a sight she and Orion made—one of the People of the Sea giving another a piggyback ride while running thirty miles an hour and carrying a golden tablet.

They entered the shade of the palm grove, the change in temperature barely registering in her bleary mind. Orion set her down with her back against the trunk of a palm tree, dropped the tablet in her lap, and pushed through the curious crowd.

Several women gathered around her, asking urgent questions in Arabic. Jaxon sighed with disappointment. If they had been Tuareg, perhaps Agerzam and his soldiers might have found her here. Instead, she was in one of those rare, remote oases in the middle of the desert. She heard the bleat of sheep and goats nearby. These people survived by grazing their animals on the oasis grass and then moving them to the next water source when the greenery got depleted.

Someone brought her water in a goatskin canteen that stank of something sour. She didn't care. She drank eagerly.

Just as she gulped down her third mouthful, the goatskin got snatched from her grasp.

Orion stood there, another goatskin in his other hand. He drained them both as she watched. The women shouted in protest, but he ignored them.

"Please," Jaxon said, her voice coming out as coarse as sandpaper. "I need more water."

"You've had enough for now. I'll give you a bit more later."

He's keeping me weak, Jaxon realized.

A couple of men came up, gripping old rifles. They didn't look hostile, just wary and curious. They asked some questions in Arabic. Orion motioned to his mouth to indicate he wanted food.

Following the timeless rules of hospitality in the desert, the group of herdsmen built a fire and started brewing up some tea. It didn't matter that their guests had come out of nowhere, unable to speak the local language and demanding rather than asking to be fed. Strangers in the desert deserved hospitality, even strangers as strange as these. One of the men pulled some flat, circular loaves of bread out of a bag, and another brought out some salted meat. A woman came up with a bag of white gunk that looked as if it might be some sort of yogurt.

Jaxon's stomach rumbled. She hadn't had any food for more than twenty-four hours. She had barely eaten before the attack, the butterflies in her stomach keeping her from feeling hungry, and after the attack, she had felt too ill. This food didn't look very clean, though. She hoped it wouldn't make her sick, as Otto had become back in Timbuktu.

She had to take that risk. This was survival.

The women tried to take her away to the women's tent, but a harsh word from Orion stopped them. So they sat together, looking like the man and wife these people no doubt thought they were, under the shade of a large canvas stretched between two palm trees, and were served together. One of the male herders squatted nearby, his rifle across his lap. They had gained these people's hospitality, but it was obvious that they had not gained their trust.

Jaxon felt grateful that Orion let her eat. He kept the water away from her, but she ate a lot of the yogurt, hoping that the moisture in it would ease her dehydration.

Orion paid her little attention, wolfing down his food and drinking so much water that one of the women had to go to the well twice to fetch more.

He was just as affected by the heat as I was, Jaxon thought. *He was able to ignore it, though. I wonder how much longer he could have gone before he collapsed.*

When they finished their meal, weariness pressed down on them. Their hosts, seeing their drooping eyelids, made motions that they should sleep and moved away to another part of the oasis.

Jaxon lay down, and Orion did the same within

reach of her. She could see him fighting sleep, his eyes closing and then snapping open to check on her.

This is my chance, she thought. *When he falls asleep, I can get out of here.*

With Orion watching her, she had to pretend to be asleep. She thought of turning her back to him, but that would only make him suspicious. So she had to face him, close her eyes, and try not to fall asleep.

After a minute, just as she felt about to be pulled under, she opened one eye, only to find Orion staring at her. She closed her eyes again.

Dream images came at her, those half visions and hints of sound that signaled the onset of true sleep. Her mind jerked her awake.

She flinched a little and opened her eyes.

Jaxon must have made a sound, because a moment later, Orion opened his eyes too.

Jaxon shut her eyes, pretending to sleep again, but knew that Orion had seen her. She decided to wait longer this time before she tried to creep away.

She didn't get that chance. Exhaustion pulled her down, and sleep took her.

Jaxon awoke with her throat on fire. She raised her heavy head and looked around. The herders were mostly at work, the young boys tending the flock, the men posted at various points around the little oasis, keeping watch, and the women and girls preparing an evening meal.

Yes, dinner already. The sun hovered low in the west. She had slept for several hours.

It felt like several days. With sluggish movements, she rose and looked around. Orion sat not far off with one of the herdsmen, having a conversation in sign language while drawing on the sand, Orion no doubt trying to figure out where they were.

A group of women sat not far off, cleaning the carcass of a goat, probably this evening's main course. She stumbled over to them, trying not to look at the open chest cavity of the goat and the bloody heap of entrails nearby that a dog was picking at. Jaxon had never realized what a privilege supermarket shopping was until this moment.

As soon as they saw her, they stood up and handed her a goatskin full of water. She hadn't even needed to ask. Jaxon slumped down and started to drink. As she did, the women sat around her, trying to block Orion's view of her. Several of the women gave her sympathetic looks and cast angry glances in Orion's direction.

Her captor stood up and looked around, quickly spotting her.

"Vacation's over," Jaxon muttered, taking another slug of water. A woman slipped her some dates, which Jaxon put in her pocket.

"We need to get going," he told her.

Jaxon got to her feet. The water had revived her, but she still felt bone weary, and her headache had not abated. The heat remained intense. She estimated it was at least a hundred degrees in the shade. She didn't want to think about the temperature out there in the sun and sand.

"Where are we going?" she asked.

"Never mind," Orion said.

"Shouldn't we wait until it's cooler?"

"No."

Jaxon sighed. She glanced over at the gold tablet wrapped in her headscarf. One of the herdsmen sat nearby with his rifle, watching them.

Suddenly, Jaxon got an idea—a terrible idea, a desperate idea, but one she had to try.

"Let me get the tablet," she told him.

He made no objection, following her a couple of steps behind.

Jaxon had to pass the herdsman to get to the tablet. His rifle lay in his lap. While he held it in a ready grip, she knew she was stronger than any regular human, even this tough wanderer of the desert.

She had never fired a gun before. In all their travels and dangers, she had avoided that stuff. Now she needed to.

Jaxon thought back to all the boasting Otto had done about the weapons training Grunt had given him, all that boasting she hadn't listened to but now had become vitally important.

A safety, she thought. *There's something called a safety on the side of the gun. You have to flick it to the open position, or the gun won't fire. But which is the open position? Does that guy have the safety off?*

He sat only a few steps away. She stared at his gun. She could see the switch right above and a little behind the trigger. She didn't see any markings on it, no helpful "on-off" written next to the switch to tell her what to do.

A little movement gave her a clue. The man's eyes narrowed as he looked past her at Orion, and the herdsman's thumb edged toward the switch.

Bingo. You have the safety on, and you're getting ready to switch it off if Orion gives you any trouble.

Sorry, buddy, but I'm the one who's going to cause trouble.

With a single fluid motion, Jaxon ducked down, wrenched the rifle from his grip, flicked off the safety switch, and spun to point the gun at Orion.

Her captor stopped. He was only a couple of steps behind her. She backed away, keeping the gun leveled at his chest.

The oasis, which had been full of happy conversation and the laughter of children, fell as silent as a tomb.

Orion did not raise his hands above his head, and he did not look frightened. He only studied her with a calculating expression.

The man she had taken the rifle from backed off, unsure what to do. What did the rules of desert hospitality dictate when one guest pulled a gun on another?

Jaxon squared her shoulders and tried to put on a brave face. After all she had been through, after all her people had been through, she still wasn't sure she could pull the trigger. Killing him was the logical thing to do, the only way to ensure she would survive and that her people had a fighting chance.

Still, she hesitated.

"Get out of here," she told Orion. "Go whichever way you like, but if I see you again, I'll shoot you."

Orion stared at her a moment then nodded.

He turned and walked away. Jaxon remembered to aim. She hadn't been doing that before. Lining up the sights, she aimed at the back of Orion's head. The gun wavered in her hands.

Orion kept going. He passed by the group of women, making a wide circle around them so Jaxon wouldn't get jumpy, and continued slowly through the palm grove.

He was halfway out of it when a baby goat scurried across his path, chased by a girl of about three.

A woman screamed. Orion scooped up the toddler and spun around to face Jaxon, using the child as a shield.

"My mission says I can kill anyone I need to in order to get you where we're going," he said. The words came out in such a matter-of-fact manner, he might have been telling her the time of day.

Jaxon slumped, defeated. She set the rifle down and stepped away from it.

Orion strode up to her, still carrying the toddler, who cooed with innocent delight and played with Orion's dreadlocks.

Orion set down the child, picked up the rifle, and

ejected all the ammunition. Tossing it aside, he grabbed her by the wrist, then he led her to the tablet and handed it to her. The nomads stared. Several had guns leveled.

"Try any more tricks like that, and I'll kill you," Orion told her with his usual lack of expression. Somehow, it felt more menacing than if he had raged and screamed at her.

He yanked her along, heading for the edge of the oasis.

A shout in Arabic made him stop. Four of the herdsmen approached, guns at the ready. One of them shouted again and gestured at Jaxon. He made his point clear by aiming his rifle at Orion's face from two paces away.

Orion let go of her wrist. Jaxon took a step away, rubbing the red marks his immensely strong fingers had left on it.

Orion stared at the nomad for a second.

Faster than she could blink, his hands whipped out, plucked the gun from his grasp, and bent it as if it were made of rubber.

He tossed the ruined weapon at his feet as the herdsmen backed off, faces pale.

Orion lunged for them, shouting at the top of his lungs.

They bolted.

Orion grabbed her wrist again, ordered her to keep up, and ran out of the oasis at what Jaxon guessed was at least forty miles an hour.

"Thank you for not killing them." Jaxon panted beside him.

"If I started to, there would have been a lot of shooting, and you might have been killed."

They ran over a series of sand dunes, and the oasis was soon lost behind them.

They kept up a brutal pace. Soon, sweat poured down her face, making her blink. The tablet in her hands seemed to get heavier and heavier.

After about an hour, she stumbled and fell.

Orion pulled out a canteen.

"Drink," he said, bending over her.

He stared.

"What's that?" he asked.

Without waiting for a response, he grabbed the gold chain around her neck that held the talisman she had uncovered in the other ruin. She had kept it hidden under her shirt the entire time, but when she fell, it had popped out from her neckline.

Orion held it up to the light. Jaxon's heart sank.

"This has power. I can feel it, just like I felt those old ruins and the tablet. I thought I was feeling you, but really, I was feeling this thing you were wearing."

He studied it for a second, examining the embossed map of the world with its strangely distorted continents and an extra continent in the middle of the Atlantic Ocean. For a moment, confusion passed over his usually expressionless features, and his eyes took on a greater intensity.

"What does it do?" Orion asked, his voice a bit shaken.

Jaxon remained silent. She took the opportunity to drink.

Orion cocked his head and looked at it a moment more then put it on.

His eyes lit up.

"Ah, I can feel them. I can feel them for miles and miles."

He slowly turned in a full circle, staring at the shimmering horizon.

"General Corbin will like this. With it, we can track all of you down."

Panicked, Jaxon leaped at him. He swung a fist into her face.

For an instant, she saw a flash and felt a sharp pain.

Then she knew no more.

CHAPTER 15

AUGUST 30, NOUAKCHOTT, MAURITANIA
11:00 A.M.

General Corbin could hardly believe his luck. You rarely got pleasant surprises in war, and he had just been handed a big one.

The local CIA official, Clifford Owen, had just told him that Vice President Salek had been picked up in a remote village and flown back to Nouakchott by helicopter. After a briefing with the Mauritanian president and his cabinet, he had called Owen to say that he wanted to come to the American embassy to speak with him and General Corbin.

That was an interesting development. Salek had

obviously heard from the police that he had made it to town and had not denounced the vice president for holding a gun to his head. The wily politician must have realized that Corbin had his own reasons for silence, that he was on some sort of mission of his own, and now Salek wanted to come over and feel him out and figure out what Corbin's intentions were.

The general smiled. Salek sure knew how to play the game. Yesterday, Corbin had dumped him in the desert and made him walk back to civilization, and now the guy was prepared to hammer out a new deal.

That suited Corbin just fine. He had nothing personal against Salek, and if the vice president proved useful, he would be happy to make a deal with him.

A deal that helped Corbin, of course.

Owen had another piece of good news. A severe storm in Senegal was keeping the American ambassador from flying back to Mauritania. Good. The last thing Corbin needed was another nosy official poking around his business.

Salek arrived half an hour later, looking none the worse for wear for his trek through the desert. No doubt he had gone back to his mansion, eaten a good meal, drunk a gallon of mineral water, and had a long sleep. A good night's sleep had revived Corbin, too, and he felt ready for the long day ahead.

And it was going to be a long, eventful day. A call to Isadore that morning assured that.

Salek arrived at Owen's office flanked by a pair of bodyguards. He was all smiles and fake concern.

"So glad to see you got out of that terrible situation, my good friend!" he said as he shook Corbin's hand while Owen stood by. "I did not see you once the attack started. How did you escape?"

"I slipped out of the prison camp while everyone was busy firing at one another," Corbin replied. "I didn't want to get captured by those vicious Tuareg bandits."

"Quite right, my friend. I did the same. You were lucky you managed to get a Jeep. I had a very long and hot walk."

Salek kept his smile as he said this, but Corbin took the hint.

"I am terribly sorry you had to suffer, Mr. Vice President. Let's sit down and discuss how we can deal with this threat and improve relations between our two nations."

The meeting that followed was a sham, and Owen was the only one there who didn't realize it. And yet the meeting was entirely for his benefit. Salek and Corbin kept up a good front, avoiding the truth about the prison camp or the real reason for Corbin's visit. The politician had obviously figured out Corbin was here without his government's blessing, and he was willing to play along. Now they shared a secret, and Corbin realized that Salek wouldn't keep that secret for free.

They discussed how to fight the Tuaregs and the People of the Sea. Owen promised more help from the CIA and better access to spy satellite photos. They also drafted messages asking for the release of General Meade and Orion to the Tuareg rebels and the "People of the Sea Liberation Front," a "terror" group Salek made up on the spur of the moment.

"I have back channels to their organization," Salek said. "I can get this message through."

Corbin had to admire his creativity and wonder what would come next when he finally got to be alone with him.

He also wondered how to ditch Owen and get that chance.

Salek solved that problem too. After an hour, he sat back and smiled at the CIA agent.

"I think we have done all we can for now. I pray to God that we get your people back safe. Now if you will excuse me, I would like to invite my good friend General Corbin to lunch at my house. We can talk over these things further."

Owen nodded. "All right. I have plenty to do here. Do you want an escort?"

Salek gave Corbin a significant look. "No, I have a good group of highly trained bodyguards. They will take very good care of your general."

"All right," Owen said, rising, then shook the vice president's hand. "I'll talk to both of you later this afternoon."

Corbin and Salek kept silent until they got out of the embassy gate. A limousine and two police cars waited outside. Several burly Mauritanian men stood around them, their eyes masked by sunglasses. Corbin had no doubt they were all armed and well trained in hand-to-hand combat.

That wouldn't save them.

Salek gestured for him to climb into the back seat of the limousine and then joined him. The plush, air-conditioned interior felt frigid after the heat of the day.

Two guards got in the front, and the little convoy moved away. Salek turned and smiled at General Corbin.

"You are a brave man to get into a car with me after what you did."

"If you wanted to hurt me, you could have told Owen everything. So what's your game?"

"*My* game?" Salek laughed. "I am more interested in *your* game. You and General Meade are here with one of the People of the Sea, and your own government does not know why. That, I find interesting. You wanted the genetic codes for the People of the Sea. At first, I thought it was for an American-government project. Now I see it is your own personal project. That is most interesting. What do you intend to do with such information?"

Corbin decided to answer Salek's question with one of his own.

"What happened to the Russians?"

Salek looked troubled. "I don't know. I haven't heard from the Russian embassy, which means either they were working on their own like you, or their government wants to deny any knowledge. This gets more and more interesting by the hour."

Corbin looked out the tinted windows at the low buildings they passed. A few other vehicles were on the road, mostly trucks and motorcycles. He kept his eye out for any Land Rovers.

"Who blew up the laboratory?" Corbin asked, pretending he didn't already know.

"I don't know. Perhaps the Russians didn't want anyone to get the information. Perhaps you blew it up yourself, eh? I see you shaking your head. Of course you deny it. Let us pretend that I believe you. Maybe you really are innocent. Luckily, not too much data was lost. We keep backups here in the capital. We lost only ten days' worth of data. We still have genetic samples for more than half of the prisoners—that's a few hundred. What would that be worth to you?"

"I can give you a good price. A few million sent to you personally, plus I can arrange more military aid for your country."

"After what happened, I am sure that will come even without your help. America is always generous with weapons. It is one of your biggest exports. No, I want something else from you."

Corbin studied him. "And what would that be?"

Salek leaned closer to him and spoke in a low, emphatic voice. "I want to be part of it."

"Part of what?"

Salek frowned. "Don't play with me. Part of whatever you're planning. I have something you need. I don't want to be bought off with a few million dollars—spare change for your government—and some outdated weapon systems your military doesn't want anymore. No. I am tired of being treated like that. You powerful countries come to places like this and demand what you want and throw us some scraps like we are beggars. An American general is missing, possibly dead, and your government will have an investigation. They will find that you were working on your own."

Corbin noticed that a Land Rover with the Doctors Without Borders logo had pulled up alongside and kept the same speed.

"So what are you proposing?" General Corbin asked.

Salek smiled. "That we join forces. We will make up a cover story together, one that will save your skin and save your project. I will vouch for you, and in return, I get to be part of your project. You have something big planned. I can tell."

General Corbin shook his head in amazement. This guy was really something else. He extended a hand. Salek shook it.

"Congratulations, Mr. Vice President. You just saved your skin as well as mine."

"I am sure we will make quite an impact."

The Land Rover swerved for them.

"Sooner than you think. Hold on!"

Corbin grabbed the back of the seat with one hand and his new partner with the other an instant before the Land Rover slammed into the limousine.

Both men flew to the other side of the limo, Salek landing on top of General Corbin. The vehicle was surrounded by gunfire. Corbin and Salek kept their heads down. The limo driver tried to pull away, but there was a flurry of shots, and they heard a loud pair of bangs as two of the tires got taken out.

The driver hit the gas anyway, grinding the exposed rims along the pavement as he tried to get his boss to safety.

Another hit from the Land Rover took care of that plan.

"Don't worry," Salek said. "This limousine is bulletproof."

Salek drew a gun from the inside of his suit. For the second time in their brief acquaintance, Corbin disarmed him.

"You won't be hurt, Mr. Vice President," Corbin said. "They're here to save me. They're making it look like a kidnapping—" Corbin stopped as several loud bangs drowned out his words "—so you just play along. I'll be in touch."

Salek grinned. "Knowing you is never dull, General Corbin."

A loud grinding sound came from nearby. Corbin saw the tip of a drill punch through the limo not far from them. Salek saw it, too, and moved away.

The drill pulled out, and for an instant, they saw some feminine fingers poke through the hole, dropping a capsule. The capsule landed on the floor, where it burst with a soft *pop*. The interior of the limo began to fill with white smoke.

"Breathe deeply, Mr. Vice President. It won't hurt us."

The world went out of focus. Before everything went black, Corbin heard Salek's voice coming as if from a thousand miles away.

"This had better be worth it."

———

General Corbin woke up to the sound of his phone ringing. He had trouble opening his eyes, and his arms and legs didn't want to obey him. For a moment, he thought he was back at his first military posting in South Korea, where as an eighteen-year-old private, he would use his one night off every other week to make a circuit of Seoul's bars with his buddies, coming back to base nine-tenths unconscious.

But he wasn't in South Korea, he realized. He was in North Africa, and he was a general now. He wasn't hungover either. He was recovering from the effects of some nerve agent he had willingly inhaled after his best assassin faked his kidnapping so he could hide the fact that he planned to overthrow the US government.

"Life comes at you fast," he mumbled, finally making it to a sitting position.

He saw he was in some dumpy back room—bare concrete walls, creaky old bed, dead cockroaches on the floor. A neatly clad Englishman he recognized as one of the McKay twins sat in an old wooden chair by the door, watching him with eyes that reminded him of a shark's. They had that same sort of soulless, dead look.

He ignored his surroundings and the psychotic killer and fumbled for his phone. It stopped ringing.

Cursing, he checked the number. Orion. Corbin had had the foresight to give him a local phone in case they got split up.

He called him back. Orion picked up on the first ring.

"I got her," he said.

"And General Meade?" Corbin asked.

"I don't know."

"Where are you?"

"A village a few miles east of Nouakchott."

Corbin blinked. "So close? How did you make it all the way here?"

"I ran."

Orion went on to give him directions on where to find them, in an abandoned house at the edge of the village. Shaking his head in wonder, Corbin told him they'd be there soon and hung up.

He turned to the Englishman, who was combing back his oily black hair.

"Which one are you, Ronnie or Reggie?"

"Reggie."

"You still have that Land Rover?"

"Got too banged up in the ruck to spin, mate. Had to scarper and pinch another."

Corbin wasn't sure what he just said. The working-class London English was hard enough to pick apart, and then the words made no sense anyway. But the guy had a vehicle, and that was all that mattered.

"We need to get going. Gather your gear, and we're moving out."

"The bobbies are as thick as fleas on a Limehouse mutt, governor."

"Whatever that means, I don't care. Get a move on."

Reggie McKay shrugged and led him out to a front room. It was a living room and kitchen all in one, obviously lived in, although he didn't see the legal residents. Corbin didn't ask. He could imagine what had happened to those poor people.

If you want to make an omelet, you have to break a few eggs, he thought, and he thought of them no more.

Isadore and Ronnie McKay sat on a sofa, obviously bored and waiting for him to wake up.

"No time for reunions," Corbin said. "Orion is half an hour's drive away. We need to go get him."

Isadore and the McKay twins were good soldiers, although certainly not his first choice of company. They got into an old car. The windows were all rolled down. Some broken glass on the driver's side told him why. He wondered what had happened to the driver and decided it didn't matter.

Half an hour and a roadblock full of dead cops later, they made it to the abandoned house by the edge of the village Orion was hiding out in.

The hypnotized Atlantean greeted him at the

doorless entrance to the crumbling old concrete building. No other houses stood nearby, and it was set back from the road by more than a hundred yards. Orion had picked his hideout well.

Orion greeted General Corbin in his usual expressionless way.

Corbin cocked his head and stared at him. "You really ran all the way here? I had to drive all night."

"Your tests are inadequate to measure my abilities."

"I see."

"I have more abilities than I realized. I can sense artifacts of power from the Atlantean times."

"Oh, you've learned your history, have you?"

"Jaxon taught me."

"She's here?"

Orion motioned to the back room and led them there.

Corbin smiled as he entered. At last, he had her again.

Jaxon lay on her back, unconscious. One side of her face was swollen, and a trickle of dried blood was caked on her chin. She did not move.

"Is she dead?" General Corbin asked.

"No," Orion replied. "But I think I hit her too

hard. It's been a few hours, and she hasn't woken up."

Corbin knelt down. He had some basic medical training thanks to the army.

"You may have given her a concussion. We have to get her to a hospital. Damn it, Orion, it might already be too late!"

CHAPTER 16

AUGUST 30, THE SAHARA DESERT, MAURITANIA
5:30 P.M.

Otto Heike couldn't stand it anymore.

After Vivian had been found knocked out and Jaxon abducted, the entire team had scoured the desert for more than a day but found no trace of Jaxon or her captor. Elaine had sent up her drone, the Tuaregs had spread out across the land they knew so well, and Otto himself had joined the search, driving until he nodded off at the wheel.

All for nothing.

"They couldn't have left in a vehicle," Agerzam

said. "All my vehicles are accounted for, and there were no tracks leading away from camp."

It was obvious how Jaxon's abductor had gotten into and out of camp—a guard had been found knocked out—but not what had happened after he had left with Jaxon. They had vanished without a trace.

"They must have left on foot, but they couldn't have gotten far," Otto said. Night had fallen, and they had reluctantly called off the search until dawn. Now they sat in a circle with only starlight to see each other. They had been playing cat and mouse with the Mauritanian Army all afternoon and didn't dare light a campfire.

Grunt rubbed his jaw. He was in bad need of a shave, and his face looked haggard with fatigue and worry. "If it was that Orion guy, they could have gotten pretty far. There was a light wind last night—not enough to erase vehicle tracks but certainly enough to erase footprints. Even if he got ten miles away, it would be hard to find him in all this desert."

"He got farther away than that," Vivian said. She sat stiffly with the others, her head swathed in bandages. "I heard him when he unzipped the tent. Before I could draw my gun, he hit me."

"I've seen how fast you draw," Otto said.

"Hit me hard too. I was out like a light."

"But how far could they have gotten?" Otto asked. "There isn't a settlement around for miles. You said so."

Grunt left the circle and came back a minute later with General Meade. He had been sitting quietly at the edge of camp, under guard, not that he really needed a guard. He was like a puppet whose strings had been cut.

"What can you tell us about Orion?" Grunt asked him.

"He was our first test subject, an American of Atlantean descent we kidnapped. We used a treatment of mind-altering drugs and hypnotism to make him a loyal slave."

Otto shuddered. To hear an American general say this so matter-of-factly made him realize just how much evil they were up against.

"So what are his capabilities?" Grunt asked.

"Strength and speed well above that of an ordinary human. We don't have much data to compare him to other Atlanteans, but he is probably better than most of them too."

"How far could he have gotten in the desert, carrying Jaxon?" Otto asked. He still held out the hope that Jaxon had been abducted, although he had been fighting a rising fear that Orion had killed her and dumped her somewhere in the desert. When they had been searching that day, every shadow of a rock made him see dead bodies.

General Meade thought for a moment.

"He can run up to fifty miles an hour and keep it up for hours, although we're not sure exactly how long. He can also tap reserves of energy, not having to eat or drink for long periods of time. We never fully tested that aspect of his abilities."

"So he could have taken her anywhere." Otto groaned.

"Yes," General Meade replied.

They all went to bed, knowing they'd have an early start and a long search the next day.

━━━

Two hours after dawn, they did find two people in the desert, although they weren't the two people they were looking for.

Otto was driving one of the Land Rovers, with Grunt in the passenger seat, scanning the landscape with a pair of binoculars. The mercenary gave a shout and pointed to their right. Otto turned the

Land Rover in that direction and, after a minute, spotted two distant figures on the horizon.

Otto slammed on the gas, and they shot over the flat desert. He leaned forward, gripping the wheel, focused on the two figures as they turned and waved their hands in the air.

He tried to ignore the fact that Orion wouldn't have done that. He tried to ignore the fact that, under their hats, the man and woman looked as if they had white skin. He so wanted it to be Jaxon and Orion that he ignored the evidence before his eyes.

Dimitri and Nadya looked half dead, their skin red and blistered, their mouths swollen with dehydration. As Otto brought the Land Rover to a stop in front of them, the two Russians held their hands above their heads.

Grunt got out, pointing his assault rifle at them. Otto aimed a pistol at Nadya through the open window. He figured she was the more dangerous of the two.

"You seen Jaxon?" he called to them.

They shook their heads.

Grunt patted them down and didn't find any weapons.

"You ran off from the fight and got lost in the desert?" the mercenary asked.

They nodded. Their mouths looked too swollen for them to speak.

Despite all these two had put him through, Otto couldn't help but feel sorry for them. Grunt put them in the back of the land Rover and gave them some water. After a few minutes, they were able to talk.

"It is as you say," Nadya croaked. "We cut through the wire at the back of the camp and ran away. Too much fighting to get a vehicle, although we did get water before we fled. We thought we would find a road, a truck, anything. We found nothing. Just sand."

Those last words came out as mournful whisper. She rested her head back on the seat and closed her eyes.

Otto continued the search pattern they had been conducting before finding the Russians. After an hour, when Nadya and Dimitri had drunk a little more and eaten some food, they had revived enough for Grunt to question them.

"So what are you two up to? Where is the rest of your team?"

Dimitri gave him a grave look. "You killed the rest of our team."

"One less problem," Grunt said. "Now answer

my other question—what are the Russians doing here?"

Dimitri and Nadya remained silent.

"Otto, stop the car."

Otto did as Grunt told him. Grunt got out, opened the back door, and dragged Nadya and Dimitri out. He locked and slammed the back door and then got back in the front.

"Go," Grunt said.

"What?"

"Go!"

Otto put the Land Rover in gear and drove off, his heart beating fast. Grunt couldn't really mean to ditch them, did he?

Dimitri ran after them, waving his hands in the air and shouting. Nadya just stood there, her head bowed.

"Let's get back to searching for Jaxon," Grunt said, scowling out the window.

"Wait. You're not really going to leave them to die, are you?"

"They're no help to us, and they're only slowing down the search. Forget them."

"No, that's not right. We have to—"

"I said forget them!" Grunt bellowed.

Otto drove for another minute, his mind in

turmoil, then he cursed and did a one-eighty, kicking up a big plume of sand.

"Where are you going?" Grunt demanded.

"Back to get them."

He didn't have the guts to look at Grunt for a moment, but when he did, he found him smiling.

"Huh?" Otto said. It wasn't the most intelligent thing to say. It just came out.

"Huh?" Grunt imitated him. "It was a test, pyro. You pass."

Otto rolled his eyes. "The things I have to put up with with you."

Grunt snickered all the way back to the Russians.

"Oh, Otto, I knew you'd never leave me," Nadya said as they let them back in. She blew him a kiss.

"Drink some more water and shut up," Otto grumbled.

Nadya smiled at him, grabbed one of the water bottles in the back seat, and took a long drink. Dimitri did the same.

"Now tell us what you know, or we really will leave you," Grunt said.

The two Russians drank some more. Otto made eye contact with them in the rearview mirror.

"You can fill your stomachs with water, but you

still won't survive this desert if we ditch you. And we will ditch you if you don't tell us what we want to know," Otto snarled, trying to sound as if he meant it.

The bluff worked. Nadya took another slug of water and replied, "Dimitri here was just a regular historian at the University of Moscow. He learned about the People of the Sea from a Mauritanian student. He started studying their culture and came across the old Saharan legends about the original water, the same water you found. He had found similar legends among the ancient Maya and the Buddhists of Tibet. That got him interested, and he found an old medieval account of a well of this water in Siberia."

"You have the water there too? Then why come here?" Otto asked.

"The well was dry," Dimitri said. "I traced the legends of the healing well. Russians used to trek three hundred kilometers to get to this well. It is still in the middle of nowhere. It took me years to find it, and when I did, it looked just like the descriptions said. It was dry, but I had at least some proof. I got one of the new oil millionaires to dig there, but we found nothing except a vast underground network of caverns, all dry."

"So you decided to look here," Otto said. "How did you get the Russian government involved?"

"They are not involved," Nadya said. "We are our own team."

Otto slammed on the brakes and brought the Land Rover to a grinding halt.

"Out!" he shouted.

Dimitri raised his hands. "All right! All right! We do have government backing. This oil baron has many connections, and he convinced the government to fund me and give me a team. They didn't believe in the water at first, saying it was just religious superstition, but someone went digging in the old Soviet archives and found more evidence for the water. Think what we could do if we got some to analyze! We could heal all illness!"

"Or make an invincible army," Grunt said. "That's what you and your government really want."

Nadya sat up straight. "Why shouldn't Russia be strong? Your government would do the same thing. That is what those American generals are after, that and the Atlantean DNA."

"That's not the government," Otto said. "They're rogue."

The Russians fell silent. Otto kept driving, making a series of crisscross paths through the desert, guided by a map Grunt was checking. The idea was to make a systematic survey of the desert and try to find Jaxon and Orion, but after what Meade had said, Otto didn't hold out much hope. Orion and Jaxon could be halfway to Morocco by then.

Or anywhere else.

Every now and then, one of the other teams radioed in to report they hadn't found them either. A couple of the Tuareg teams had been chased by the Mauritanian military, which had shown up in large numbers, and the rebels warned everyone to be on their guard.

Nadya and Dimitri started whispering to each other in Russian.

"Quiet back there," Grunt said.

They fell silent. After a minute, Nadya spoke.

"Let's make a deal."

"You have nothing to bargain with," Grunt replied.

"We have the Russian network in this region. They can help you find your friend."

"Oh yeah, have the Russian government find Jaxon—that would really make everything better," Otto said.

"You will never find her this way, and soon, you

will have to call off the search when the army comes after you."

Otto and Grunt glanced at each other.

Nadya went on. "We have failed to get the water, and we cannot get the secret from you. The next best thing for us to do is to stop those American generals. If we cannot get what we want, at least we can keep the enemy from getting what they want. We have agents all over the region. If you let us contact them, we can start the search. Even if they go to another country, we can find them. They are a very visible pair."

Otto and Grunt glanced at one another again.

"How can we trust you?" Otto asked.

"You can trust that we don't want those generals to succeed. We have to come back to our government with something."

Otto grinned. "Or you'll be back in Siberia, but this time not looking for a healing well."

Nadya pouted. "Oh, Otto, you used to be so nice to me."

Grunt glanced between him and the Russian spy.

Before he could ask any awkward questions, Otto said, "You'll try to betray us the first chance you get."

Nadya laughed. "Of course we will, you silly boy! Your bald friend with the funny tattoos already understands this."

Grunt tried to hide a smirk. Otto rolled his eyes. He just couldn't win with these people.

"Do we risk it?" Otto asked Grunt.

Grunt shrugged. "What do we have to lose?"

"Plenty."

"Not really. They're right—we're not going to find them, and if we keep looking, we're going to get busted. All of us. Then it's game over."

Otto thought for a moment, trying to figure out a better way, a safer way, a way that didn't require them to trust people they knew were untrustworthy.

He couldn't come up with anything.

CHAPTER 17

SEPTEMBER 1, ROSSO, ON THE BORDER
BETWEEN MAURITANIA AND SENEGAL
3:15 P.M.

General Corbin watched as Isadore prepared the syringe. Nearby, Jaxon lay in a hotel bed in a state of chemically induced unconsciousness. Her head was wrapped in fresh bandages. Vice President Salek had been kind enough to send a top doctor from the capital to take care of Jaxon's concussion. A good thing, too, because Corbin didn't trust any of the doctors in this hick border town.

They had been here for two days, waiting for Jaxon to heal. She was recovering much faster than an average human but still needed time. Keeping her unconscious had proven to be the only way to keep her in line. Any time she regained consciousness, she screamed and fought. Corbin didn't want to have to kill her, at least not yet.

They had moved south to this border town on the Senegal River on a hunch. While Jaxon was still severely injured and drifting in and out of consciousness, she had mumbled something about the Gambia. Corbin had no idea what was going on in that nation, just three hundred miles south of there, but he decided to get as close as he could while still being able to rely on Salek's help. Once they left Mauritania, they'd be on their own.

"You sure the truth serum will work on an Atlantean?" Corbin asked.

Isadore shrugged. "I have no idea. I can double the dose if you want."

"Do it."

"That might have adverse side effects," Isadore warned.

"She's not as valuable as she once was."

"All right." Isadore added some more serum and set the hypodermic next to another one that would wake up Jaxon.

Before she gave her the injections, Isadore handcuffed Jaxon to the metal frame of the bed.

Corbin drew a pistol, a gift from Salek, and kept it ready.

"Will those cuffs hold her?" he asked.

"She might be able to break them, but she'd break her arm doing it. She's still only flesh and blood," the assassin replied.

Isadore gave Jaxon the first injection, telling Corbin it would take a few minutes to wake her up.

Impatient, he moved to the balcony of their hotel, the best in town but still pretty run-down. It did have a fine view, though, over the low concrete and wooden buildings and three or four minarets to the gleaming river to the south. On the far shore lay Senegal, and beyond that the Gambia. The air was more humid here, and trees grew along the sides of the streets. The people were different, too, fewer of the brown-skinned Arabs and Tuaregs and more black-skinned Africans from south of the Sahara.

He'd been monitoring the news. His and General Meade's disappearance had become international headlines. The government hadn't been able to keep it out of the papers. It didn't matter. Salek was already concocting a story about his being kidnapped by the People of the Sea. Corbin had even posed for a video, tied to a chair and with Orion posing next to him with a gun. It all looked very convincing. Salek would release it when the time was right and then go on to "save" Corbin. That would make Salek a hero and get him loads of support from the United States, and Corbin's story about investigating an Atlantean terror group would be vindicated.

Of course, that meant Salek would have even more dirt on him. Corbin didn't like the idea of that guy knowing so much. Once he got in power in the United States, he'd have to take care of him. Of course, that wouldn't prove easy. Salek would no doubt share his secrets with a few trusted advisors or leave the information in a safety deposit box in some European bank, to be released to the media on the occasion of Salek's death or disappearance. That was standard insurance practice in the underworld, and Corbin had no doubt Salek would think of it. Corbin would have to tread carefully.

That would all come at a later time. Right now, he was happy to be invisible, using the false passport he had kept hidden in an inside pocket of his uniform all this time. Now, he wore civilian clothes and traveled under a different name. He just hoped no one recognized him. His face had been plastered everywhere.

"She's coming to," Isadore said.

General Corbin moved back to the foot of the bed and pointed his pistol at Jaxon. The teenager's eyes fluttered open. The first thing she saw was the black muzzle of the gun. Her eyes widened with a brief spike of fear then narrowed in anger and calculation.

"You awake enough to listen?" Corbin asked.

Jaxon nodded, wincing at the pain the simple movement caused her.

"Good. Behave, and you might make it out alive."

"I don't have much hope of that," Jaxon replied. Her voice came out weak.

"You could have had so much if you had just stayed with us," Isadore said, giving her the second injection.

Jaxon watched her warily. After a minute, her eyes glazed over and her mouth went slack.

Corbin had used truth serums before. Unlike what they showed in the movies, a truth serum did not force the subject to tell everything. They still had some willpower. What it did do was lower their inhibitions and their rational thinking, very much like being drunk but with the memory and intelligence intact. It took careful questioning to get around the remaining resistance and extract the needed information.

General Corbin and Isadore were both trained in finding out just what they wanted in these circumstances, and after an hour of poking and prodding and asking the same questions over and over again in different ways, they found out everything they needed to know.

And what they learned changed everything.

Both Jaxon and Orion had more power than he had suspected, and some strange old artifact down in the Gambia would give them more. Once he had assembled enough Atlantean slaves, he could shift the artifact from one to the other, using their various special abilities at will. He would have unlimited power.

He realized that he had been too modest in his aspirations. Why rule the United States when he could rule the world? It was possible now.

But first, he had to get down to the Gambia and get that artifact.

"We should kill her," Isadore said once she had given Jaxon another injection to knock her out again. "Let me give her a poison. I can make it look like a heart attack. Rare in someone her age, but the doctors here won't suspect a thing. She's too much of a danger to bring along."

Corbin rubbed his jaw, considering. "She *is* a bit of a handful."

"She's been nothing but trouble since the beginning. She's got too much of a mind of her own. I offered her wealth, and she turned her back on it like it was nothing."

"There are more things in the world than money."

Isadore kept a neutral expression. Corbin knew that if he hadn't been her boss, she would have laughed right in his face. It didn't matter. Power was far more important than money, and he'd have plenty of that soon enough.

"Let me kill her," she repeated. "We have Orion. He can sense where the artifact is."

Corbin paused and looked at the little black bag that contained Isadore's collection of poisons sitting on the bedside table. Just a single little needle jab, and one of his major problems would be solved forever.

"No," he said at last. "It's better to have two of these special Atlanteans. What if something happens to Orion? Then we'll never get that artifact. Besides, once we get her back to the Poseidon Project, we can get her under control."

Isadore shook her head. "Don't be too sure."

"We shall see. If she causes too much trouble, we can always kill her later. Right now, though, we have to plan a trip down to the Gambia."

Luckily, his good friend Vice President Salek had already provided them with a large Land Rover that could hold them all. It was a bit cramped, and Corbin didn't really like to share his space with a pair of psychopathic twins, an assassin, a slave, and a prisoner, but he didn't want a second vehicle. He didn't want to split up his forces. Corbin had the feeling that the Atlantis Allegiance wouldn't be far behind.

▭

The trip down to Banjul, the capital of the Gambia, took two days. The roads were bad and clogged with trucks, and the lines at both border crossings took hours. Customs officials in this part of the world took ages to check every vehicle and get through the paperwork. Corbin sweated every minute of the way. He had to beat the Atlantis Allegiance down here, or all would be lost. He made frequent calls to Salek for updates, but the vice president could tell him little. Besides some battles with the Tuaregs, who now had People of the Sea fighting in their ranks, there was no sign of the troublemakers.

That prison camp was getting some international attention, though. Video of the squalid conditions had made it onto the Internet, and while the major news media usually ignored human rights abuses in countries they didn't care about, the story gained extra interest since two American generals had disappeared in the same country. The press speculated that the two events might be linked, but they had no proof.

Corbin barely noticed the beautiful countryside they passed through. After crossing the Senegal River, they had left the desert behind. Soon, the land became lush, and they passed grasslands waving in the wind, palm trees, and fields of millet. The people were mostly black Africans and far more numerous than up north. Villages of thatched-roof huts dotted the road every few miles, and the radio was alive with dozens of stations rather than a couple of faint, distant broadcasts.

On the afternoon of the second day, they got to Banjul, a bustling city of half a million people near the mouth of the River Gambia. While Jaxon's description of the Atlantean slave trader had been vague, it had been enough to track down some information on the Internet. Mars Sans Pitié had been quite a colorful figure in the seventeenth century. He had, for a brief period, dominated the mouth of the River Gambia, one of the main outlets for the slave trade. His fort still stood just a few miles downstream from Banjul.

General Corbin wasted no time going there. They grabbed the first livable hotel they could find and headed for the riverside. Unfortunately, he had to bring Jaxon along. He needed all his people at the fort, and he didn't dare knock her out and leave her alone in the hotel room. If she woke up, she'd cause all sorts of trouble. Her Atlantean body had healed far more quickly than a normal human's, and she was full of fight again.

The McKay twins got her in line.

"Listen, lass. You cause a ruck or try to scarper, we'll be hard on you."

"I'll behave," Jaxon said. Corbin wasn't convinced. Neither were the McKay twins.

"You remember our razors, luvvie?" one of them said.

Jaxon nodded soberly.

"Well, if you make a fuss, we'll skin the ears off the nearest babe and feed them to his mum on toast. Understand?"

Jaxon shuddered. She knew they meant it. Good. Corbin didn't want that sort of spectacle on the streets of Banjul.

And those streets were far too crowded for his liking. They had to shoulder their way through a thick crowd. The dirt roads were a cacophony of honking trucks and revving motorcycles, and what passed for the sidewalks were lined with little wooden market stalls selling peanuts, bananas, jugs of palm oil, and cheap Chinese electronics and plastics. Locals, mostly young men, kept pestering them.

"You need hotel?"

"No."

"You need guide? I show you the market!"

"We're already walking through it."

"You want to buy some bananas?"

"Do I look like I do?"

"Yes! Here is a good bunch. Very cheap!"

Ronnie McKay pushed the banana seller out of the way.

"You need hotel?"

"I already told your friend I didn't."

"You want bar? I know a good bar."

"I'm beginning to need one, but no."

"You need boat?"

That got Corbin's attention. He kept on walking

but actually looked at the guy who tagged along beside him—a lanky teenager in denim shorts, leather sandals, and a T-shirt that had more holes than fabric.

"You have a boat that can fit all of us?" Corbin asked dubiously.

"My uncle's boat! Very fine boat. He can show you everything—the port, the bay, he can even take you all the way out to the ocean for fishing."

"We only want to go to one place. Can he take us to the fort of Mars Sans Pitié?"

"Of course! He give you grand tour. You learn everything. He knows everything about Mars Sans Pitié."

Corbin didn't go on many vacations, but he knew a tourist hustle when he saw one. It didn't matter. He needed a boat, and if this wiseacre could actually get him one, that was good enough.

By the time they made it to the riverside, Corbin's civilian clothes were stuck to his body with sweat. It was almost as hot here as Mauritania, with about a hundred percent humidity. The McKay twins must have been broiling in their jackets and ties, but nothing got those two to change into different attire.

The boat turned out to be an oversized wooden

canoe called a *cayuco*, a common mode of transport in West Africa. It looked stable enough for river work, and it could hold up to ten people. A whole row of them lay beached on the river, and dozens more plied the waters, carrying people and cargo.

"Kid, you got yourself a deal."

The teenager's uncle was a wiry old man who studied his customers with a sharp eye. Corbin had to admit they made a strange sight. The boatman's gaze rested on Orion and Jaxon for a moment, and he asked a question in a language Corbin couldn't identify, let alone understand.

"You speak English?" Corbin demanded.

The boatman turned to him but kept glancing at the Atlanteans.

"A little, yes."

"We'd like to go to the fort of Mars Sans Pitié."

The boatman turned and spat on the sand.

"Why you want to go there?"

"Never mind that. I'm willing to pay well, and I'm willing to pay in dollars."

They agreed on a price that was far too high for a Third World boat trip, but Corbin was too impatient to haggle.

Corbin and his team climbed aboard, and the

boatman and the teenager pushed the *cayuco* into the water, hopped in, and grabbed some oars.

The current was strong, and they made good time, soon leaving the city behind. The river grew wider, and they smelled the ocean not far to the west. Villages and isolated farms and fishing shacks lined the shore. Fishing boats and ferries plied the river. A freighter moved slowly by, heading for the port in Banjul.

"Too many people," Isadore grumbled.

Corbin nodded. He had just been thinking the same thing.

"We get this done as quickly and quietly as possible," he whispered to her, "and if your former foster daughter causes any trouble, get rid of her."

Soon, they came to the island where Mars Sans Pitié had built his fort, too soon for General Corbin's liking. They were still in a populated area of the river and only half an hour from the outskirts of the capital.

The island stood near the south shore, a small, rocky outcropping rising above the muddy water. The fort's stone walls looked well-preserved. They made a rectangle about two hundred yards to a side with triangular bastions at each corner. A few rusty cannons poked from the ramparts, still covering the approach up the river.

The fisherman and teenager steered the boat toward the island. As they drew closer, Orion stirred.

"It's there. I can feel it."

Corbin glanced at Jaxon. She didn't even notice as she stared at the island.

They drew closer. Corbin saw a chain-link fence running around the island right where the water met the stone.

"It's closed?" Corbin said.

"They are developing for tourists. It open in a year."

"Oh great. Take us around the whole island."

They made a slow circuit of the island. The fort took up much of the space except for the southern part of the island, where there was an open area and a small jetty. A couple of *cayucos* were docked there, and some workmen were clearing away underbrush and repairing a section of the wall that had crumbled. Much of the fort was overgrown on this side, where a bit of soil clung to the rocks and gave life to vines and bushes. The plant life had created cracks in the walls. Vines and creepers crisscrossed the stone.

"Bring us in," Corbin ordered.

"It is not allowed."

"Damn it, do as I say!"

"Witnesses," Isadore murmured.

Corbin ground his teeth. "Fine, don't go in."

The boatman hadn't turned toward the jetty anyway.

Isadore leaned over to her boss. "We'll come back at night after the workmen are gone."

Corbin nodded his assent, if not his approval. They took a slow turn around the island. At least two dozen workmen were busy restoring the fort, and Corbin noticed a small shack with two soldiers lounging in front. Great.

A cluster of wildflowers grew in a large tuft at one end of the island, a brilliant display of reds, purples, and yellows. Bees as large as horseflies buzzed around it. Some flew out over the water, and one passed close to the boat.

The McKay twins panicked.

"Get it away! Get it away!" they shrieked, leaping around the boat while the unsuspecting bee circled lazily around. The *cayuco* rocked, and the boatman shouted for them to sit down.

"What the hell is the matter with them?" Corbin demanded.

"You didn't know?" Isadore asked, trying to pull

the twins back into their seats. "They're afraid of bees."

"Lunatics!" Corbin said, raising his hands in the air. "I'm working with lunatics."

Jaxon sat in the stern of the boat, watching the commotion with a contented smile.

At last, the bee buzzed away, the twins calmed down, and the boatman paddled upstream.

"Whoops, there's another bee," Jaxon said.

"Where?" the twins demanded, jumping up again.

Isadore smacked her upside the head, but that only made her giggle.

Once they got back to Banjul, they sat down in their hotel and tried to figure out what to do. Jaxon lay unconscious on one of the beds. Isadore had given her an injection so she wouldn't overhear anything.

"You sure it's there?" Corbin asked Orion.

"Yes. It's an object of power from Atlantis, like that pendant and gold tablet I gave you. I felt it. Jaxon felt it too. I could tell."

"We'll get a boat tonight and go over there. It looked like only a couple of soldiers guard the place. We can overpower them easily enough."

Isadore shook her head. "We can't, not tonight."

"Why the hell not?" Corbin demanded.

"Because we're not ready. We have to plan how to take over the island long enough that we can excavate and find whatever is there. Who knows? It might be under ten tons of rock. We need digging equipment and an escape plan. We need to figure out an escape route back to Mauritania or a flight to Europe. We also need to figure out what to do with her," Isadore said, jabbing a thumb in Jaxon's direction.

"I can sort that if you're feeling queasy," Ronnie McKay said.

"And then we have a body on our hands. No, at least not yet. We'll have to get rid of her eventually, but we're going to need all day tomorrow to get everything ready. Then we can hit the fort tomorrow night."

"But we're so close!" General Corbin raged.

"All the more reason not to get in a hurry," Isadore said. "The Atlantis Allegiance has no idea where we are. We're safe for the moment. But as soon as we kill a couple of Gambian soldiers and break into a historic site, we're going to have a police investigation on our hands. Let's not rush the job when we're almost at the end."

Corbin ground his teeth and didn't reply. She

was right. He was getting too anxious, too hasty. That was a bad thing to do in the field. Some jobs needed time and planning. This was too important to rush in with no clear direction.

"All right," he said with a sigh. "Let's sleep on it and get everything ready tomorrow. We'll hit the fort tomorrow night."

———

So they had no choice but to stay in Banjul and get rest before a long, dangerous day. Corbin found he couldn't rest and went out to a bar down the street from his hotel in order to have a drink or two before turning in.

His hotel was on one of the main streets in Banjul's downtown, and here he saw something he had never seen in Mauritania—tourists. Fat, sunburned sheep with cameras. Corbin detested tourists. There was nothing wrong with taking time off if you needed a break, but aimlessly taking photos of distant places while not learning a thing about those places seemed to him a massive waste of time. It turned out the Gambia was a resort for mostly French tourists who came down for the pristine beaches on the Atlantic coast. That seemed to

Corbin to be an even greater waste of time. The south of France had some of the best beaches in the world, so why fly all that way to go to a different one?

He dismissed the tourists from his thoughts and decided to ignore them, but that turned out to be a mistake.

Corbin sat in a bar in a mixed crowd of locals and tourists, listening to African pop music and sipping a delightfully cold beer. He felt grateful to have gotten to a country where alcohol was legal. He mulled over his options, trying to figure out how to get into that fort. He did not notice the sunburned, middle-aged Frenchman staring at him from a table on the other side of the room.

Alphonse Gardinier was no one special, just a middle-management businessman on holiday. A nobody, really, and he knew it. He had a colorless job and a humdrum life in a Paris suburb. Occasionally, he splurged on an exotic vacation to have a little excitement outside his usual routine, but otherwise, his life was pretty dull and unimportant. Perhaps that was why he was such an avid reader of the newspapers. He wanted to see what the important people were up to, to keep up on the great events of the world. *Le Monde* was his favorite newspaper, a conservative, reliable source of information that didn't challenge his preconceived ideas. He had been reading *Le Monde* every day for years and had even written a couple of letters to the editor, sharing his thoughts on French elections. The paper hadn't published them.

So of course Alphonse Gardinier had heard the story of the two missing American generals and had seen their photos on the front page. So it was with some surprise that he saw a somewhat haggard, sunburned man who looked an awful lot like General Arnold Corbin drinking a beer at a bar in Banjul.

Could it really be the same man? He thought the general had been killed or captured by terrorists. This man didn't look like a prisoner.

The French businessman watched him for a while, unable to decide if this was the same man or not. Then the man ordered a second beer, and when he did so, he ordered in English.

American English.

Alphonse Gardinier was a nobody, but every now and then, it was the nobodies of the world who changed the course of history. The Frenchman lifted up his phone and snapped a photo.

He smiled. If he was correct, he would be famous, at least for a day or two. If he wasn't, it would make a funny story to tell his friends. The journalists at *Le Monde* would have to figure out the man's identity for themselves.

Alphonse Gardinier returned to his hotel room to use the Wi-Fi and send the image to France's biggest newspaper. Then he went to sleep, having no idea that he had, for a moment, become the most influential person on the planet.

CHAPTER 18

SEPTEMBER 4, BANJUL, THE GAMBIA
11:00 P.M.

"You're coming with us," Orion said, taking the handcuffs off Jaxon and motioning for her to get off the bed.

Jaxon sat up, her head spinning. Those drugs Isadore kept giving her made her sluggish and dizzy. She'd been asleep for most of the day and had trouble remembering what had happened since she had been captured.

She could remember one thing, though.

When they had ridden in the boat the day before, she had sensed that the Atlantean artifact was somewhere in the fort on that island. The key to

Mars Sans Pitié's power lay hidden beneath its stones.

The Atlantean slaver had created a little empire with nothing more than his own powers, but General Corbin would have a whole army of Atlanteans under his command. He'd be able to do anything.

Jaxon stood, holding onto the headboard for support. She needed to get her head together. She was the only person standing between Corbin and everything he wanted.

But she had seen some things on that island that had given her ideas.

"Don't cause trouble," Orion ordered. "If you do, you'll be killed. And remember what that Englishman said. He'll kill some children out of spite."

"Doesn't it bother you to be working with people like that?"

Orion shrugged. "I do what I'm told."

Unlike the desert cities to the north, Banjul stayed up late, and they had to push through the crowd to get to the riverside. After dark, the sidewalks turned from markets into cafes, and the locals, mostly men, sat out in the temperate evening, sipping coffees and talking over the day's events. Jaxon stared at these people as she passed, wondering what would happen to countries like theirs once Corbin got in power. She knew he wouldn't be satisfied with only ruling the United States. He would aim for world domination, and with an Atlantean army behind him, he might just get it.

Then another terrible thought came to her. Even if he didn't win, even if a coalition of countries eventually defeated him, her people would be looked on as dangerous enemies by the rest of the world. They'd be even more oppressed than they already were.

Orion walked close beside her, holding her hand in a firm grip. She knew at any moment, he could tighten that grip and snap her fingers. The McKay twins walked close behind her. Corbin and Isadore walked in front, Corbin carrying a heavy duffel bag that clanked as it shifted. Jaxon was held and boxed in. How could she do anything to stop all this?

She would try, even if it meant her death. She had no more illusions. If Corbin found the artifact, she wouldn't be necessary anymore. She wouldn't live to see the dawn.

Panic welled up inside her, but she forced it down and concentrated on slowing her breathing. Ironically, she used a yoga breathing technique

Isadore had taught her back in California when she was pretending to be her foster mother instead of her guard.

The crowds, the cafes, the blaring music all seemed surreal as they walked to the river. Panic threatened to take her over again, but she forced her mind to clear and worked on her breathing.

You're not dead yet, she told herself. *On the boat trip, you noticed things. You noticed vines and bees and lots of flowers.*

They passed down one of Banjul's few paved roads. She saw a tuft of grass had broken through the pavement, nature reclaiming its place in the face of civilization.

You noticed that too. You have a chance. Just breathe, be calm, and wait for the right moment.

At the riverside, they found a fisherman stowing away his nets. Corbin offered him some money to take them out on the water.

Once they got away from the lights of the city and were alone on the quiet river, one of the McKay twins slashed the fisherman's throat and dumped him in the water.

The panic returned. Jaxon closed her eyes and tried to breathe.

When she opened them again a few minutes

later, she saw the McKay twins at the oars, while Corbin and Isadore both sat facing her, guns drawn.

"Better cuff her before we get there," the general said.

Isadore nodded and moved over to Jaxon, who did not resist as Isadore put her hands behind her back and handcuffed them.

Why don't they kill me and dump me in the water like that poor fisherman? Jaxon wondered. *Are they going to keep me for experiments? Or maybe they want to make sure they get the artifact first. Perhaps Corbin doesn't trust Orion's abilities and wants me as insurance.*

The island and fort of Mars Sans Pitié loomed up before them, a dark shadow against the moonlit glow of the river. Corbin turned to Orion.

"You remember where those soldiers are?"

"Yes."

"Go take care of them. Do it quietly and then signal us."

Orion stripped down to his shorts and dove into the water. Within seconds, he had disappeared into the darkness.

The McKay twins gave him time. They rowed slowly around the island, well away from shore, and came to the southern side.

A soft sound came over the water. Had it been a cry of pain? It was too faint and cut off too quickly to tell. After a minute, they heard a sharp whistle come out of the darkness. The McKay twins rowed to the island.

Jaxon took a deep breath.

Here we go.

They bumped against the rocky beach, and Orion appeared out of the shadows and pulled the boat onto dry land with all of them in it.

Everyone clambered out, Isadore helping Jaxon since she couldn't use her hands.

The island was quiet except for the buzzing of insects. Dimly, Jaxon could see the guards' shed not far off. Two darker shadows lay like inkblots in front of it. None of the others took any notice as they led her up a small path through the overgrowth to the crumbled wall of the fort.

This part of the wall had all but fallen down, and a heap of rubble gave them an access ramp up to the top of the cracked parapet. Orion had to carry Jaxon up the steep and shifting slope.

Once at the top, they stopped to rest. Orion put her on her feet, and they looked around the fort, the stone shining softly in the moonlight.

It was a large rectangle, with triangular bastions

that stuck out from each corner like arrowheads. The interior was mostly empty except for the foundations of a few buildings that had probably once housed the soldiers.

Jaxon could feel the presence of the Atlantean artifact. It was at the other end of the fort and a little down, perhaps in a cellar or hidden cist. Orion sensed it too. He stared in the exact same direction she did.

A little way along the catwalk, past a rusty cannon, a flight of stone steps led down to the courtyard.

Orion got in front and led them down the stairs and across the courtyard to where a doorway opened, as black as the maw of some nightmare monster.

Isadore produced four flashlights and shared them with Corbin and the McKay twins. They shone the light through the doorway.

What they saw there almost made Jaxon scream.

Beyond the doorway stood a large, arched room. The back half was sectioned off with heavy iron bars reaching from floor to ceiling. A small gate with a heavy lock was the only way through. Chains and manacles hung from the back wall.

"A slave pen," Jaxon whispered.

Peering around, they saw that to the left of the

cell, a passageway continued into the darkness. It felt as if the artifact was in that direction. Orion led them that way.

Jaxon got in front of him. Orion stopped. She couldn't point with her hands secured behind her back, so she jabbed her chin in the direction of the slave pen.

"See that? That's what Mars Sans Pitié did with his power. He enslaved people, including our people, and sold them like products. Is that what you want?"

Something flickered in Orion's face for a moment, a trace of emotion. An instant later, it was gone.

Orion merely shrugged.

"You won't get far with him," General Corbin said and laughed.

"Yeah, you've already enslaved him, and now you want to enslave the rest of us!" Jaxon shouted.

"Keep your voice down, kid, or I'll have Isadore gag you. As for being enslaved, the American people are already enslaved. They're slaves to their televisions and advertising and consumerism and their easy lifestyle. They're slaves to their ignorance and weakness, and all the time, they're talking about how free they are. When I'm in charge, we'll have order, and we'll make the people strong again. Sure, they'll still be slaves, but at least they'll be slaves who accomplish something. I'll do great things for the country and the world. You think we can solve problems like the terrorism threat and the environmental crisis with a weak and divided government voted in by an ignorant populace?"

Jaxon scoffed. "You trying to tell me you're doing all this to save the whales?"

General Corbin smiled. "Environmental degradation is a threat to national security. I'm no tree hugger, just a pragmatist. If a species goes extinct, we can't exploit it anymore. Too much pollution, and we get lung cancer, no matter how rich and powerful we are. But enough talk—let's dig up whatever is here. I want my place in history, and Isadore here wants to be the richest woman on the planet. The McKay twins will get a nice bonus too."

"You're doing all this for money?" Jaxon asked her former foster mother.

Isadore's eyes shone. "Billions."

They moved down the corridor, startling a few mice, which scuttled away from their lights and footsteps. The passage turned, opening up into a small room. Moonlight shone through slits in the walls from which the guards would have once fired guns.

Their flashlights settled on a spiral staircase at one corner of the room, heading down.

At its bottom, they came to a large, vaulted cellar. Their flashlights could not penetrate to the far end. From somewhere unseen came the sound of dripping water. The air was dank, and moss grew on parts of the wall and floor. A few tendrils of vines poked through here and there. Nature was trying to reclaim this sad place.

She could feel the artifact. It wasn't far off. They moved a little through the darkness and saw the rest of the cellar. It was featureless and empty, probably once a storehouse for weapons or food or slaves. Along one wall, she saw a row of rusty shackles. Not far beyond that, she knew, lay the artifact.

Orion hurried over to the spot. He stood on a flat stone floor, staring down at his feet.

"It's right below me," he said. "But I don't see any sort of seam or opening. It looks like Mars Sans Pitié set these stone blocks and mortared them together to keep anyone from knowing where his artifact was."

"Then how could he get at it?" Isadore asked.

Corbin shrugged. "Maybe with a power we don't know about. Let's get to it."

Corbin and Isadore set down their duffel bags,

opened them, and pulled out picks and shovels. One of the McKay twins gestured at Jaxon to move over to the wall where the shackles were.

"You set there, luvvie, and don't move a bloody muscle. Pity them chains are too blighted to snap onto you."

Jaxon did as she was told. The twins moved over to where the others stood and took the picks Corbin was handing out. Isadore pulled a pistol and stood in front of Jaxon.

"Any trouble, and you know what happens," Isadore told her.

The men got to work. The cellar echoed with the clink of iron on stone as they hacked their way through the floor.

Jaxon rested her back against the cold wall, old slave shackles lying to either side of her. Her hands, cuffed behind her back, groped around the stone. She felt a smooth, damp bed of moss right by her. Studying the wall, she saw a few roots of creepers had pushed through, seeking out water. Plants could push through anything, given time. She had always known that but had not really thought about it before.

Orion and the McKay twins smacked at the stone with the picks, breaking off pieces that Corbin shoveled away. They made good time, Orion doing more work than the other three combined.

It wasn't long until they got down to what they were looking for.

A final stroke of the pick, and instead of the sharp crack of metal chipping stone, she heard an echoing thud as it broke through into a cavity below. Corbin ordered a halt and peered through the hole with a flashlight.

"It's there. Careful not to hit it."

The men resumed their work, chipping away at the edge of the hole. Jaxon looked away. The scene was too distracting, and she needed to focus. She pressed her hand against the moss and felt a tingling in her palm as she began to pass some of her energy to the plant. She felt it grow and spread, still hidden behind her back so that Isadore could not see it.

Jaxon concentrated on what she wanted. She had never tried something this complex before. Plant tendrils popped through the wall behind her, the little sound masked by the digging nearby.

The tendrils brushed against her wrists, tickling her as they worked their way to the handcuffs. She imagined them moving into the keyhole then expanding to work the lock and open it.

For a moment, nothing happened. The tendrils

grew thicker, and she heard a soft metallic creak, but the cuffs did not open.

Corbin knelt over the hole in the floor and reached inside, the flashlight illuminating his eager face.

"I got it!" he cried out.

The sound of his voice masked the sound of the handcuffs opening and falling off her wrists. Isadore looked over at her boss as he pulled out a small wooden chest. Corbin opened it, eyes wide, and pulled out a thin circlet of gold. It reminded Jaxon of paintings she had seen from the Middle Ages. Nobility used to wear them around their heads.

Now or never, Jaxon thought.

She summoned her strength, pressing both hands against the moss on the wall. She disregarded her safety, her limits, as she brought forth the power of all the plants nearby.

A strange crackling came from the walls and floor as green tendrils burst through. Her captors cried out, looking all around in wonder.

Isadore was the first to figure out what was going on. She turned and pointed her pistol at Jaxon.

Too late. The tendrils shot out of the ground all around the assassin, wrapping around her body like a net. They dragged her down as she fired a single shot. The bullet pinged off the wall, and the sound of the gun echoed through the cellar.

Then she was held firmly on the floor, and she couldn't fire again.

The others were having equal trouble. The McKay twins slashed at the tendrils with their razors but couldn't get entirely free. Corbin struggled as two thick vines wrapped around his wrists, keeping him from drawing his gun.

The thickest tendrils wrapped around Orion, breaking through the stone floor to encase his feet, twine up his legs, and grab his arms.

Orion's muscles heaved, and with a great tearing sound, he broke free. A second later, more plants shot up to grab him, and he had to stop to rip them apart as well.

Jaxon's head spun, and she realized she had already overtaxed her energy. She was surprised she had been able to do this much. Back in the desert, making a single seed bloom had nearly knocked her out.

But that had been an ancient seed, preserved for millennia in the desert sands, and she had been in the dead land of the Sahara Desert. Here, there was moisture and soil and plants eager to grow. She wasn't bringing anything to life—she was merely encouraging them.

Even so, she couldn't keep this up for much longer, and when she faltered, Orion would break free and kill her.

She jumped to her feet and ran for Corbin. She had to get that gold circlet.

One of the McKay twins leaped forward, nicking her in the side with his razor before the plants pulled him back. Jaxon winced and kept going. Orion saw where she was headed and moved for Corbin too, fighting plants every step of the way.

Jaxon got there first, barely. She grabbed the circlet and yanked it out of the general's grasp.

Then she ran.

She ran out of the cellar, the sound of tearing plants echoing through the dank stone room. She ran into darkness, the flashlights of her captors a receding pool of light behind her.

The cellar rang with the sound of a gunshot, and a bullet cracked against the stone some distance to her right. Three more shots chased her, but now that she had plunged into the shadows, whoever was firing had to fire blind.

She slammed into a wall, fumbled along it, and

found the spiral staircase upward. She felt weak and light-headed from the exertion of using her powers, but she couldn't stop now. Fear gave energy to her legs.

Jaxon stumbled up the stairs as flashlight beams probed the darkness behind her, searching for her.

When she came to the top of the stairs, she entered full darkness. Her captors, who could see, would soon catch up to her. Moving by memory and feel, she hurried down the corridor as swiftly as she dared and entered the slave pen, where some feeble moonlight filtered in from the open doorway.

She made for it, burst into the courtyard, and desperately looked around her.

On the opposite corner of the fort stood one of the bastions, overgrown with ivy and other plants. It had partially crumbled, and nature had taken over. Bushes grew on its sides, anchored to the old stone, and flowers bloomed out of crevices in the rock. A doorway beneath it led into darkness.

She ran for it, half tripping from weakness, and made it into the shadow of the doorway just as the flashlights shone in the slave pen behind her.

Jaxon stepped farther into the shadows of the doorway, her breath coming in great, panicked gusts. She sensed an open space behind her, a room, perhaps, but with no light, she didn't dare move any farther inside. There could be snakes or a hole in the floor or any number of other dangers.

Her pursuers emerged from the opposite doorway. Orion came first, then Corbin and Isadore with pistols in their hands. The McKay twins strode calmly after them, their straight razors gleaming in the moonlight.

They stopped in the middle of the courtyard and looked around, searching for her.

"I'll find her," Orion said.

He reached into his pocket and pulled out the Atlantean pendant that helped a Keeper of the Texts find his people.

As Orion put it around his neck, Jaxon put on the circlet.

And everything changed.

Suddenly, she felt no more fatigue, no more fear. Suddenly, she could feel every plant on this island, felt as if she had roots seeking water, and leaves catching the breeze, and flower petals folded up for the night, awaiting the sunrise to open again.

And she knew that she had power over all of them.

No, power was the wrong word, because she didn't really control them. She merely guided their growth.

And grow they did.

The bushes growing on the bastion spread to make a dense thicket to shield her, and the vines extended and shot forward like snakes, reaching for those who would do her people harm.

Her pursuers cried out and scattered in every direction. Jaxon focused and sent the vines after them as more vines crawled up the walls on all sides of the fort to join in the fight.

The McKay twins, who had run together, got caught on a staircase leading up to the wall. They got back to back and slashed with their razors at the plants coming at them from above and below. It was all they could do to keep free. They didn't have a moment to spare to move toward Jaxon.

Isadore had made for the slave pen, seeking the closest shelter, when a vine caught her ankle and made her fall. The vine dragged her back to the center of the courtyard, where several more vines wrapped around her.

Corbin guessed where Jaxon was hiding and fired several shots at the thicket screening the door. Bullets thunked into thick branches and snipped off leaves. One bullet made it through and hit the doorway inches from Jaxon, spitting fragments of stone into her face.

Before Corbin could fire any more shots, a wave of greenery swept over and buried him.

Orion did not have to guess where she hid. With the pendant around his neck, her fellow Atlantean looked right at her and ran for the bastion.

She focused on him, sending a host of vines to grab at his limbs. His remarkable strength matched theirs, and while they caught him, he was able to break free. His charge slowed to a crawl.

Yet he still moved forward.

Jaxon redoubled her efforts, sending more vines to trip him and grab him, but still he moved for her, narrowing the space between them inch by inch. Out of the corner of her eye, she noticed the others begin to break free. She couldn't focus on them while expending so much effort to stop Orion. The McKay twins began to hack their way down the stairs, back to the courtyard. Isadore managed to fire a poorly aimed shot at the bastion before once again having to fight the vines. Corbin heaved up from beneath the shrub holding him down, looking like some little grassy hill convulsing in a miniature earthquake.

She couldn't deal with them now. They would still need some time to get to her. They weren't a threat for a few more seconds. Perhaps she could stop Orion by then.

And still he approached, a determined look on his face. Jaxon focused her energies, and Orion had to stop as he fought off a dozen vines coming at him from all sides.

He did not stop long. After a few seconds, he took another step forward, fought off another onslaught, and then took another step. He was almost to the screen of bushes now, Jaxon's last defense.

The McKay twins got free first, cutting through the last of the vines with their razors. They bolted across the courtyard, ignoring the struggles of Isadore and Corbin, and made their way straight for Jaxon's bastion.

She sent a final wave of vines at all three of them and turned her attention to the screen of bushes.

She made their branches intertwine into a thick wall with only a few little gaps to see through. Then she made them bloom all over with flowers, urging their petals to open to the night. Suddenly, the entire fort became immersed in their sweet fragrance.

The three murderous men coming at her didn't seem to notice. Orion made it to the wall of bushes and began to tear through. A few seconds later, the McKay twins joined him and hacked at the branches. In another minute, they'd be hacking at her.

A soft buzzing came to her ears, growing in strength. The island's bees had caught the unaccustomed whiff of nighttime flowers and rushed to gather their nectar. Within moments, the space on the other side of the wall of bushes swarmed with bees. The McKay twins screamed in utter terror and bolted.

That left only Orion. He tore at the bushes, widening a hole he had already made and ignoring the occasional bee sting. Beyond, Jaxon could see Isadore and General Corbin slowly freeing themselves.

She gritted her teeth and focused once again. The hole in the bushes began to close as Orion had to turn his attention to fighting off another onslaught of vines and creepers. He flailed around like a man electrocuted, continually jerking both his arms and legs to yank them free from the plants' grasp.

Out of the corner of her eye, Jaxon saw Isadore finally break free, run over to Corbin, and help him tear away from the last of the clutching plants. She had no energy to spare to trap them again. It was all she could do to hold off Orion.

Plants came at him from all sides—from the

ground, from the walls, even from the arch of the doorway behind which Jaxon hid. Stone cracked and chipped as more plants broke through, and part of the old exterior wall nearby crumbled as more vines crawled over it.

That gave Jaxon an idea. Heart racing, stomach churning, she focused on the plants just above her, the vines that clung to the arch of the doorway and the walls just inside. She made them grow, broadening their roots. Stone cracked as the relentless strength of nature asserted itself.

Orion did not notice. Freed from the attack, he tore at Jaxon's protective wall, opening a gap that he began to push through. The plants fought back, delaying him, but he was stronger. Jaxon stepped back into the dark interior of the room, stumbling over something that made a metallic clank as she hit it. Another shackle from the time of slavery?

She didn't have time to look. Orion broke through the barrier and stumbled into the doorway.

At that moment, the arch of the doorway collapsed.

With a resounding crash, hundreds of pounds of stone fell right on him, burying him in an instant.

Jaxon brought her hand to her mouth in shock. She blinked as the dust and grit settled, and the last fragments of stone fell away. Not all of the room had collapsed, only the area around the doorway, only the area Jaxon knew Orion would step into.

Orion had disappeared. The stones completely covered him.

She had buried him.

She had killed him.

Her stomach clenched, and Jaxon felt the urge to throw up.

Then self-preservation kicked in.

Corbin and Isadore raised their pistols. Now that the barrier of plants had been torn away and the entryway caved in, Jaxon stood in full view in the moonlight.

She leaped to her left just as they fired. She felt a hot pain lance along her side as she stumbled into the darkness. A faint glimmer of moonlight guided her, and she ended up in an adjoining room, one with an old cannon poking out a gun port.

Jaxon rushed to it, heaved the cannon out of the way, and squeezed out the gun port.

She gasped with relief to see a vine clinging to the side of the wall right next to the opening. Grabbing it, she willed it to move upward, and it pulled her to the top of the wall.

She peeked into the courtyard. No one.

Isadore and Corbin must be just below, searching for her. For sure, they heard her move that cannon. But where were the McKay twins?

A movement in the river caught her eye. Two distant figures were swimming for the far shore. Good. Two fewer enemies.

A sound from below reminded her that she still had two very dangerous ones to face. She scampered along the wall, looking for a place to hide. Even with all her powers, bullets moved faster than plants. She needed to surprise them.

She found a spot between the wall and an old cannon that was wreathed in shadow. Crouching behind the cannon, she looked out over the fort.

It had completely transformed. It looked as if it had spent a hundred years being reclaimed by a jungle, at least the half closest to her. The walls, one bastion, and much of the courtyard were covered in vines. She could see cleared areas where her captors had cut their way through. The moonlight made it look surreal, like some living carpet.

Her side began to sting. She checked it and found the bullet had plowed a furrow right below her ribs, but it hadn't gone in deep, and the blood didn't flow freely. It only welled up slowly. She'd be all right for the moment.

Despite her situation, Jaxon couldn't help but smile. She remembered once, in sixth grade, she had cut her finger with a pair of scissors in art class and nearly fainted at the sight of a few drops of blood. Now she was shrugging off bullet wounds.

Just as she was about to look out across the fort, the moon passed behind a cloud. Glancing up, she saw that great, puffy clouds floated in from the sea, the moonlight shining behind them making them look like spun silver.

That would look beautiful if it weren't endangering my life, Jaxon thought.

A soft step brought her attention to her left. She probed the darkness with her eyes, desperate to spot her attackers before they found her.

After a moment, she saw a shadow shift. The stairway to access this side of the fort's wall was about fifty yards away. Someone crept up it.

Jaxon waited until the shadow made it to the top of the catwalk and the person paused to look around. They started to move in her direction, stepping quietly over the mat of vines that draped over the wall and catwalk, whoever it was still obviously not seeing her but guessing that she hadn't had time to flee to the opposite side of the fort.

Jaxon focused, and the vines heaved up and

engulfed the person. She heard a short feminine cry before Isadore's voice got muffled in a cocoon of greenery.

Silence. The moon still hid behind a large cloud. Corbin would be close, and she knew she'd better shift her position before the light came back. She peered into the shadows and saw no one, heard nothing but the faint rustling of the vines as Isadore tried in vain to break free.

Jaxon stepped out from behind the cannon, headed for the far end of the fort. She had the circlet. If she could get to the boat, she could get out of there. Or she could swim. If the McKay twins could reach the shore, so could she.

She only made it three steps before a gun roared from a shadow. She felt a hard punch to her chest and a sudden lightness, and the world spun.

Jaxon ended up on her back. She did not feel much pain, more shock. The moon came out from behind a cloud. It looked beautiful.

A shadow blotted it out. General Corbin.

"I'll get you out in a minute, Isadore!" he called over his shoulder then turned to Jaxon.

"It's called a feint. You pretend to attack in one direction while your real strike comes from another.

You just learned that little bit of tactical wisdom the hard way, and it's the last thing you'll ever learn."

Corbin began to blur. Coldness spread out from Jaxon's chest.

General Corbin bent down and pulled the circlet off her head.

"You won't be needing this," he said. "But I most certainly shall."

CHAPTER 19

SEPTEMBER 5, ON THE RIVER NEAR BANJUL, THE GAMBIA

1:30 A.M.

Jaxon moaned as Corbin yanked the circlet off her head. The sound came out pitiful, hopeless. All this work, all this struggle, and she had lost.

Her people had lost.

"You were a good fighter," General Corbin said, taking a step back and pointing his pistol at her face. "Too bad you were on the wrong side."

Jaxon looked back at the moon, framed by silvery clouds. After so much ugliness in her life, she wanted the last thing she saw to be something beautiful.

A gunshot. Jaxon jerked ...

But did not die.

General Corbin fell to the ground with a heavy thud. The gold circlet rolled out of his grasp and ended up by Jaxon's hand.

Grunt stepped out of the shadows, gripping a Kalashnikov.

Elaine rushed over to Jaxon's side.

"You made it," Jaxon said, her voice coming out so faint that she herself could barely hear it.

"I hope we're not too late," Elaine said, examining her wounds.

Jaxon managed to point at the circlet. "Put this on."

Elaine did as she was asked and then placed her hands on Jaxon's chest.

Soothing warmth spread through her cold body, and the strange sensation of her bullet wounds closing up, her ribs reknitting, and blood filling up her veins and arteries.

"Ah!" Jaxon cried, and sat up. It had been even more powerful than the water.

She looked around her, still in a state of shock. General Corbin lay nearby. Grunt stared down at him with a grim expression. Otto rushed to her side, and they kissed. Everyone else was here too.

"How did you find me?" Jaxon asked, clinging tightly to Otto.

"A French newspaper published a photo of General Corbin at a bar here in Banjul. We saw it on the Internet. The journalists weren't sure if it was the missing general who's been all over the news or not, but we were sure."

"But you got here so fast. It took us two days from the Mauritanian border."

Otto laughed. "Nadya and Dimitri got us a Russian Army helicopter. We made it in three hours. Now they're gone. I guess we won't see them anymore."

Otto sounded relieved.

"You got here just in the nick of time," Jaxon said, turning to Elaine, who still had the circlet on her head. "Wait! There's someone else you need to heal."

She got to her feet, found she had as much energy as if she had just awoken from a good night's sleep, and rushed to the overgrown bastion where she had made her stand. Her blood-drenched clothes left an ugly trail of drops behind her. Her friends followed.

Jaxon stopped at the pile of rubble.

"I buried Orion under there," she said.

"Good riddance," Mateo replied. "He was a traitor to our people."

"He was enslaved with drugs and hypnosis!" Jaxon objected.

Elaine and Winston began to remove the rubble.

"This is a bad idea," Mateo said.

"I agree," Grunt added, pointing his gun at the pile.

The two Atlanteans cleared away the stones from Orion's head and shoulders. Even in the pale moonlight, he made a sickening sight—crushed and bloody.

"I'm not sure, even with this thing on, I can cure him," Elaine said.

"Keep him pinned under the rocks like that," Grunt said. "If he tries anything, I'll shoot him."

"I'll heal him a little bit," Elaine said. "Winston, once I do, you can try to reason with him."

"All right."

Elaine touched Orion's face.

"Still a little life left," she whispered and closed her eyes in concentration.

Orion's face shifted. The broken jaw realigned, and the partially crushed skull went back to its proper shape with a sickening crunch. He let out a soft moan, and his eyes fluttered open.

Elaine stepped back. "Wow. He was so close to death I could never have done that on my own." She removed the circlet and held it out to Winston. "Take it. You'll be able to do anything with this."

Winston took a step back. "That's what I'm afraid of."

Jaxon put a hand on his shoulder. "It's all right. I trust you."

Winston gave the circlet a wary look. "I'm not sure I trust myself."

"Your power only works on people temporarily. You won't be able to save Orion without it."

"Why should we save him at all?" Mateo asked.

"Because he's one of us!" Jaxon snapped and turned back to Winston. "Or he will be if you help him. It's all right."

Winston sighed, took the circlet, and put it on his head.

"Oh," he whispered. "I can feel the power."

He stepped closer to Orion and looked down at him. Unlike all the other times Jaxon had seen him move minds, Winston did not soothe him with kind words, did not try to persuade him with nice phrases, as you would a child.

In fact, he didn't say anything at all.

Winston just looked at him.

Jaxon did not need to be told that it had worked. It was obvious. Orion's features completely changed. His face took on awareness and intelligence she had never seen before. He looked around him, shock and relief mingling in his eyes.

Then he burst into tears.

"The things I've done!"

Jaxon knelt beside him. "Were not your fault. You're free now."

Orion nodded, but Jaxon could tell he would carry the burden of all those murders for the rest of his life. She patted him on the shoulder. At least she wouldn't carry the burden of his murder.

"Let's get these rocks off him so I can finish healing him," Elaine said. "Winston, help me ... Winston?"

Winston had taken a step away from the others. He stared at them with intensity that frightened Jaxon. His face twisted, and she could see him forcing himself to be calm. He snatched the circlet off his head and tossed it to Jaxon.

"Suddenly, I saw myself as the king of my own kingdom," Winston said through labored breaths. "Just like Mars Sans Pitié. Everyone would have bent to my will. I could have had anything—devoted followers, women, anything. That thing should only be used by a Keeper of the Texts. Only they have the wisdom to use it right."

"Wisdom? I don't have any wisdom," Jaxon said.

"You had enough wisdom to save a fellow Atlantean who tried to kill us all," Elaine said, kneeling next to Orion again. "Winston's right. That thing is too much of a temptation. I can heal him with my own power."

And she did, nearly knocking herself out from the effort. As a grateful Orion laid her down to rest and began asking her all about their heritage, Grunt and Vivian checked the fort for anyone else who needed healing. Sadly, the two Gambian soldiers guarding the place were dead. Isadore was still trapped in a cocoon of plants.

"What should we do with her?" Vivian asked. "We need to get out of here. Someone is bound to have heard those shots. The police will be on their way."

Grunt laughed. "Let's leave her. I already reached through the vines and disarmed her." He cupped his hands and faced the section of wall where she was trapped. "Sorry, honey, but you're going to have to wait in there a bit. Good luck explaining to the Gambian police about all the bodies and plants and everything. I'm sure the jails here are very luxurious. Just the kind of place you always wanted to live in. Bye-bye, now!"

Snickering, he led the others to a couple of *cayucos* beached on the shore next to the one Corbin stole.

"There's a gold tablet with Atlantean script we found in the desert," Jaxon suddenly remembered. "It's in our hotel."

"We'll get it." Grunt nodded as everyone got into the boats. Suddenly, he looked up the river. "Oh damn."

A couple of motorboats were swiftly approaching, police lights spinning on top of them.

They pushed off and paddled like mad for the nearest shore.

"Why is it that every time we're trying to save the world, we end up getting chased by the cops?" Jaxon asked.

"Welcome to the life, my friend." Grunt laughed.

No, Jaxon realized. *This isn't my life anymore. We've won.*

The realization came with a mixture of triumph and sadness. The Atlantis Allegiance had formed to help her and to defeat the secret plot within the US government. Now that they'd achieved that, there was no more reason for it to exist. She suddenly knew that these people who had become so dear to her in the past few months would soon go their separate ways.

She paddled for shore, the line of trees and huts blurring with her tears.

Two days later, the inevitable came. Jaxon stood in front of Banjul's small airport as the members of the Atlantis Allegiance got ready to depart. The Atlantis Guard would stay with her, and with the items they had, they could reunite their people. Perhaps they could even find a translation for the tablet they had retrieved.

General Meade had been ditched in Banjul. Despite some reservations, in the end, they had decided not to cure him. In this state, he would no longer be a threat to anyone, and to lose some of his mental faculties was a small punishment for all the people he had hurt. Dr. Yamazaki had made a call back to the Poseidon Project and warned them of the danger that was headed their way. Dr. Jones had promised to destroy all the evidence. They hadn't done this to let Dr. Jones off the hook, but to get rid of any information that could hurt the descendants of Atlantis. Sadly, like the McKay twins, Dr. Jones was one of the many guilty people who would go free. Jaxon had learned the sad lesson that justice wasn't always served out to those who deserved it. It was just another sad fact of life.

Like the fact that many of her friends were leaving. They had all made plans for their future, and judging from how quickly they had announced them, she got the impression that they'd been planning for this end for some time now.

Dr. Yuhle shook her hand. "Good luck to you. And if you ever need any help on the scientific front, get in touch."

"That goes for me too," Dr. Yamazaki said, giving her a peck on the cheek. "We're both going back to the States to look for work. You can look us up easily enough."

"Thank you for everything," Jaxon said. She had never been terribly close to either of them, but now it pained her to think they would no longer be around.

"Take care of yourself, honey," Vivian said.

"You sure you want to go back there?" Jaxon said. The mercenary was the only one not flying to the United States. Instead, she was heading back to Mauritania.

Vivian shrugged. "The Tuaregs could use my

help." Then she smiled. "Plus, Agerzam and I have a bit of a history I'd like to repeat."

Jaxon laughed. "Yeah, I noticed that!" She grew serious. "Try to see my people there, and try to explain to them that I never meant to cause so much trouble."

"I will," Vivian said.

She gave her a big hug. As they separated, they both had to wipe away tears.

"Don't be too sad, kid," Grunt said, giving her a bear hug that nearly snapped her spine. "You're going on a whirlwind tour of the world, and this time, you're not going to have to keep looking behind your back."

"I wish you guys were coming with us," Jaxon said.

"This is your job now. You've found your place, and you've found your family. But don't be a stranger, eh?"

"I'll see you guys again," Jaxon said, and she knew it was true. But it didn't make her miss them any less. They were going on different paths, moving on to different phases of their lives.

She turned to Otto, who stood uncertainly nearby. Her first boyfriend. Now he was becoming her first breakup.

"I'm going to miss you," Otto said.

"You can always come," Jaxon said, not really sure if she wanted him to or not.

Otto gave her his winning grin, the one that so attracted her to him back in that group home. He elbowed Grunt. "Nah, I have to keep this big lunk out of trouble. He says he wants to give up the mercenary life. I'll have to stick around to make sure he does."

"Good luck to you both," Jaxon said.

Jaxon couldn't quite sort out her feelings. She would miss him terribly and at the same time felt a bit relieved. She had dated him because he was the first guy to show any interest, and while she respected and liked him, she had something more to focus on right now. Even as recently as a few weeks ago, she would have been too insecure to let him go. Now she could say goodbye, knowing he wasn't the one and wouldn't be the last.

Jaxon noticed that they were alone. Everyone had discreetly moved into the airport. She took the opportunity to give him a proper kiss goodbye.

After they finished, she pushed him gently on the chest.

"Now get out of here before I start blubbering

like a baby," Jaxon said. *Or you do,* she thought when she saw the look on his face.

She returned to the Land Rover, where the Atlantis Guard waited for her. Mateo was at the wheel, the passenger seat empty for her. In the back sat Winston and Elaine. Her new family. The first three of many.

As she got in, Mateo looked past her at the airport terminal.

"You know, they weren't bad for humans."

"They were the best," Jaxon said, wiping her eyes.

Mateo looked at her. "You ready?"

"Yes. Where to?"

"You're the Keeper of the Texts. You're in charge."

Jaxon laughed. "I've dodged responsibility all my life, and now it looks like I've inherited it."

"You can manage it," Winston said.

Jaxon thought for a moment. "The Gambia is just a thin little bit of land on either side of the river. I looked at the map, and there's a road along the river that goes the entire length of the country. This is the perfect place to start looking for our people. If we drive up that road, I'll sense every Atlantean in the country."

Mateo nodded. "Sounds like a plan. Then we have to figure out what country to do next."

"We'll do them one by one until we've contacted all of our people."

Mateo grinned. "You're more patient than I am."

Jaxon smiled back at him. Yes, even with the pendant, it would take years to go to every country and contact everyone. It would take a lifetime.

A lifetime with purpose. A lifetime of doing something important for the community of which she was a part. That was what she had been missing growing up.

Now she had it.

The Land Rover drove out of the airport parking lot, heading for the main highway. Even though she would miss the people she had left behind in the terminal, she did not look back.

She had too much to look forward to.

CHAPTER 20

SIX MONTHS *later in Los Angeles, California ...*

Dr. Yamazaki stared at the DNA sequence on her screen, trying to puzzle out a recessive trait she had recently isolated. Every few seconds, she looked out her office window at the grassy quad in the biotech section of UCLA, the bright California sun blazing on the neatly manicured grass and modernist sculptures. Beyond the quad stood the glass-and-steel buildings of the chemistry and botany departments.

She couldn't concentrate.

Dr. Yamazaki looked at her screen again, trying to tease out the details of the chromosomes, and found her eyes straying back to the quad.

She had been here four months, with a prominent post at the genetics department and some promising research, but she found her mind always straying back to other places, other times.

The bright sun and blue skies reminded her of the North African desert, although they were a pale reflection of that blinding canopy under which she had enjoyed the adventure of her life. She fiddled with a rock she had on her desk. Just a bit of black basalt, nothing special, but she had picked it up in that old fort and put it in her pocket. It had never been far from her since.

Of course, she had been keeping track of developments and trading emails on the Dark Web with other former members of the Atlantis Allegiance, but it wasn't the same. She had gone back to being the same meticulous, quiet scientist she had been before this whole thing began.

None of her new colleagues had any idea that she had once jumped a Saharan wadi with the Mauritanian police on her tail, or that she had helped excavate archaeological sites from the lost continent of Atlantis. None of her new colleagues had any idea that she had, for a brief period of time, been a heroine.

It scared her a bit, how quickly she had fallen back into her old life. How quickly she had become normal again. But her memories of that other life weren't really what kept her from her work that day.

It was the knowledge that she was going to get a visitor.

After another hour of sitting in front of the computer and not getting any work done, he finally came.

A knock on the door, and her shy, unassuming colleague came through the door.

Yuhle looked different. It took a moment to figure out what had changed.

Actually, three things.

First, he had a look of intensity on his face, determination that had so rarely shown itself even in the toughest times. He had always been the quiet one, maintaining his cool when times were toughest, getting by with gentle persistence. He did not look like that now.

He had also changed physically. Yuhle had been soft before, the typical science nerd, although the desert had hardened him. To her surprise, he had hardened even more. He was obviously spending as much time in the gym as the lab.

"What happened to your glasses?" Dr. Yamazaki asked, pointing out the least important change about him.

Yuhle laughed, but not his usual self-deprecating laugh. It was more casual.

"Those? I got contact lenses. Those glasses never fit me anyway."

"So how is Berkeley working out for you?"

"San Francisco is great. I love the beach, although really, I should be so sick of sand that I should move to Ireland for the rest of my life. The institute has been really supportive. I'm getting good funding for my research, and this time, there aren't any high-level government conspiracies to stand in my way."

"You know you're always welcome here. I'm heading my own research project, and I could really use your help."

"Well..." At this point, Yuhle put his finger on the bridge of his nose as if adjusting his now-vanished pair of glasses. "I prefer to have my own place these days. You see, Akiko, I think it's best if we aren't working together."

Yamazaki felt a flush go over her. "Really? I always thought we worked well together."

"We did," he replied, almost touching the bridge of his nose again but stopping himself at the last moment. "I just think we need to move on."

"Oh."

Yamazaki's gaze strayed out the window. She struggled to find the words. Yuhle saved her by going on.

"What I'm trying to say is that I think it's best if we are free from the constraints of university rules."

Yamazaki's gaze flicked back to him. Briefly, their eyes met. Yuhle looked away first.

"Is that from the fort?" he said, looking at her desk.

"Yes."

"I picked up some sand from Mauritania," he said, meeting her eyes again.

There was a long pause. This time, Yamazaki looked away first.

"What I mean to say..." Yuhle started then took a few seconds to collect himself. "What I mean to say is that we shouldn't be constrained by university rules about personal life."

Yamazaki's breath caught. She tried to speak and couldn't. Her old coworker seemed to be having the same problem. At last, she summoned the words.

"You mean you want to work in separate institutes so we can..."

She didn't have the courage to finish her sentence, but she did have the courage to get out of her seat and take the two steps to cross her office to stop right in front of him.

And Yuhle had the courage to kiss her.

And in Rabat, Morocco ...

The peace negotiations were almost finished. Agerzam and Daouda Ndiaye, representing the Tuaregs and the People of the Sea, had finally come to terms with the government of Mauritania, with the help of the governments of Morocco and the United States, both of which wanted to see stability in the region. As the delegates gathered their papers at the end of a hard day's work, everyone seemed buoyed by optimism for the future. Once the treaty was finalized the next day, the Tuaregs and the People of the Sea would have equal rights in Mauritania, guaranteed by a new constitution and overseen by a United Nations task force.

Vivian smiled at Agerzam. She had become his partner, both at the negotiating table and in other places. She had discovered she had a talent for negotiation and smoothing out the tricky details of legal treaties. Some of the United Nations delegates had already suggested she might find work in their organization.

She had told them she would consider it. While life as a mercenary had been fun, she had learned that there were other ways to solve the world's problems.

Of course, you couldn't make the world perfect, she reminded herself as former Vice President Salek crossed the room to shake their hands. He was now President Salek, raised to power after a palace coup, and now the ruler of Mauritania. The old trickster had managed to cover up all participation in the plot with General Corbin.

Now he was all smiles.

"I am so glad we have come to this agreement," he said, shaking each of their hands in turn. "I predict a bright future for our people."

"There will be if next year's elections come off as planned," Vivian said.

"Of course! It is my most cherished dream to see full, true democracy restored after the terrible events of the past year," the new president said.

Agerzam managed to smile, as did Daouda Ndiaye. They both knew that Salek would run for reelection and could get more votes than any candidate they could put forward. He'd become quite popular both at home and abroad, with the reputation as a peacemaker and moderate. He'd pardoned the prison commandant and his men, gotten millions in foreign aid, much of it for the important voting bloc of the military, and brought renewed stability to the nation by agreeing to a ceasefire and peace talks.

And of course, he had made sure everyone knew about it.

Vivian wanted to wash her hand after shaking his.

After a few more pointless pleasantries, they headed out the door and back to their private offices. The griot said he was tired and wanted to rest, and the various assistants scurried off to their work, so soon, Agerzam and Vivian were alone.

"Ugh! I can't stand that guy," Vivian said. "Can you believe he's the president now?"

Agerzam let out a weary chuckle. "I'm surprised he didn't become president sooner. I'm afraid we're stuck with him."

"We can't trust him."

"We can trust his greed. Daouda Ndiaye says he is like a blade of grass, blowing with the wind. He can survive the storms of the desert much better than a hard branch that will not bend and only ends up breaking in the wind. Salek is getting everything he wants—power, prominence, wealth, a place in the history books..."

" And immunity from prosecution," Vivian finished his sentence.

Agerzam shrugged. "No one is even trying to prosecute him. He covers his tracks better than a Tuareg warrior being chased by enemies."

Vivian shook her head, and Agerzam ran his fingers through her blonde tresses.

"I still think it's a shame we have to grin and work with that guy, pretending everything is all right," Vivian grumbled.

"We could have far worse, and we have had far worse. Right now, Salek's best interests happen to coincide with ours. In time, he will see a country at peace is more prosperous than a country suffering from civil war. That will line his pockets and make him more popular with the common people. I suspect he will win many elections."

Vivian gave him a hug. "You're the real winner, you and Daouda Ndiaye. You've brought peace and equal rights to your people."

Agerzam returned her hug then held her at arm's length and studied her face.

"I have heard those UN delegates speaking to

you about a job in Washington. Are you going to accept?"

"Do you want me to?"

"No."

"Then what will I do for work? I'm tired of being a mercenary."

"The Tuaregs will need an ambassador at the UN. That position must go to a Tuareg, of course, but the ambassador could use an experienced Westerner who has seen so much of the world and has a talent for negotiation."

"But I'm not a Mauritanian citizen."

A slow smile spread across Agerzam's face. "That can be solved quite easily."

Vivian smiled back at him. "Then I accept."

And in the Sonoran Desert, Arizona ...

Otto pounded the last of the fence posts into the hard Arizona earth and wiped his brow. He'd finally finished. Once he placed the horizontal rails in place, they'd have a new corral for the horses.

He paused for a moment, looking out over the beautiful Sonoran Desert with its red rocks and mesquite trees, its rough mountains and tall cacti that looked like green men standing at attention. This was the kind of desert he could grow to love. It wasn't dead like the Sahara but remarkably alive. He spotted a rabbit scampering through the underbrush, and at night, he could hear the coyotes howl from the nearby peaks.

It was a peaceful place to live, the first peaceful place he ever had.

"Hey, pyro!" Grunt bellowed from the barn that stood behind the little ranch house a couple hundred yards from where Otto worked. "You want to go riding, or do you want to set fire to the desert?"

Well, mostly peaceful.

"I pick riding," Otto called back.

"Good choice. I'll get the horses."

"I'll help."

Otto climbed the low hill to the barn to find Grunt inside, already saddling the two mares he had purchased along with the house. Grunt had saved up a lot of money during his career as a mercenary, and he now had his dream home.

"You going to apply at University of Arizona?" Grunt asked.

"Tomorrow," Otto said with a nod. Tucson was

only half an hour's drive away over the mountains through Starr Pass Trail.

"Figured out what you are going to major in?" Grunt asked as he cinched up the saddle strap. Otto got a saddle and put it on the other horse.

"Archaeology."

Grunt inclined his head. "Never took you for the academic type."

"I never was until I found out history could be so interesting."

They rode out of the barn together.

Grunt asked, "You thinking of helping out the Atlantis Guard with their excavations? Of maybe getting back together with Jaxon?"

Otto laughed and shook his head. "They don't need my help, and as for Jaxon, I think she's got her own future to think about."

"You came along at the right time for her."

"I suppose, but that time has passed. I hope I gave her a little bit of confidence."

"You did."

They headed out onto a narrow trail through the prickly pear and agave.

"I was her first boyfriend, you know. First kiss, even."

Grunt looked sidelong at him. "First anything else?"

"No."

Grunt nodded. "That's probably for the best."

"Yeah," Otto sighed. "I miss her sometimes, though. I miss all of them."

"So do I, pyro. But that's how life is—you gotta appreciate the people you have while you have them."

They headed up a faint trail that led up a nearby hill. A mile beyond lay a narrow canyon with some beautifully striated red-and-yellow rock layers and towering spires. It was one of their favorite places to ride.

"So what are *you* going to do?" Otto asked. "You'll get bored sitting in the desert all day."

"A little bit of boredom would do me some good right about now. I've been shooting up the bad guys for so long, I'm sick of it. I'm never going to be a mercenary again."

Otto laughed. "Oh, is that why we have a small arsenal hidden under the barn?"

Grunt grinned. "Life insurance, pyro. You never know what the world might throw at you."

"Don't I know it."

Grunt surveyed the land around him as they

came to the crest of the hill. The canyon lay past a wide, flat area cut by a couple of arroyos. "Ranching. Maybe I'll take up ranching. This part would be good grazing ground. It's pretty well watered."

"That will take a lot of work. I'll help out after class and on weekends."

"Yeah, when you're not catting around with those co-eds! It's okay, pyro. It will be fun to build something for a change."

"Well, if you want to do it all by yourself, I can get a part-time job in town, help pay for expenses."

Grunt punched him in the shoulder. "You don't have to pay to live in your own house, son."

Otto smiled back at him. "Thanks, Dad."

And in the Bahamas ...

Jaxon Ares Anderson lay on a beach towel spread across the brilliant white sand of a Caribbean beach, the sun bathing her closed eyelids with warmth. After she had left the Sahara, she had sworn she would never step on sand again, but she could make an exception for this.

In the past six months, she and the Atlantis

Guard had visited ten countries, going to every continent except Antarctica. They had journeyed as far south as the southern tip of Chile and as far north as Iceland, connecting with her people. With the Atlantean artifacts they had uncovered, it proved easy. She knew where all the Atlanteans were in a region even before the plane landed. They found families and even small communities here and there, but mostly, they found lone individuals, people as ignorant of their past as she had once been. And now they were all learning and all getting in touch with one another.

The Caribbean was their current stop. It had been a trading outpost in ancient times, and there were still many Atlanteans here, but Jaxon was in no hurry to find them. She deserved a break for a few days.

Besides, she had plenty of company already.

The Atlantis Guard had grown. In nearly every country they visited, they found people who wanted to join them in their travels and help find other lost members of their community. Some were computer experts who set up secure servers so Atlanteans in different countries could talk to one another. Others were healers or specialists in ancient history. They had found several more inscriptions, and a team was busy piecing the ancient Atlantean language back together. They hoped to crack the code by the end of the year.

She opened her eyes and looked at the beach around her. More than twenty of her people lay nearby or splashed in the water. Elaine lay next to her. They had become close in the past few months, and Jaxon was beginning to look at her more like an aunt or a big sister than a friend. She needed someone like that. Winston lay not far off. His calm words had been a great reassurance to her during the trip. Mateo and Orion played volleyball a little way down the beach. They had become good friends.

It had been a wonderful trip, and it would continue for years to come. She didn't mind not having a place to call home. She had been moved around all her life. The difference was that now, she took her home with her and belonged wherever she went.

She smiled and closed her eyes again.

After a minute, she heard someone calling out, "Sunscreen! Beach blankets! Frisbees! Sunscreen! Beach blankets! Frisbees!"

It was one of the many local teens who worked on the beach, selling things to tourists. A Frisbee would be nice. She got up on one elbow, spotted the teen not far off, and waved to him.

He looked about seventeen, a lanky kid in Bermuda shorts and a faded T-shirt. He was dark-skinned like most locals, but as he approached, she noticed that he had wide Asian features and sparkling blue eyes.

She also noticed that he was very, very cute.

"I'd like a Frisbee," she called out.

He came up to her and smiled.

"You have blue eyes like me," he said.

"What's your name?"

"Noah."

"Look around you, Noah."

He did, his jaw dropping as several pairs of blue eyes looked back at him from wide, dark faces.

"Whoa."

"Where's your family, Noah?" Jaxon asked.

His face fell. "I grew up in an orphanage. I don't have a family."

Jaxon patted the towel. "Yes, you do, and it's right here. How about you sit down and we'll talk."

Noah inclined his head. "With a pretty girl like you, I'd be happy to sit all day."

The teen sat down, and Jaxon began to tell him things that would change his life forever.

ABOUT THE AUTHOR

S.A. Beck lives in sunny California. When she's not surfing, knitting or daydreaming in a hammock, she's writing novels.

www.sabeckbooks.com